D0149681

THE GUILTY

THe GUILTY

Juan Villoro

TRANSLATED BY KIMI TRAUBE

STORIES

GEORGE BRAZILLER
New York

Copyright © Juan Villoro 2015
Translation Copyright © George Braziller 2015

All rights reserved. No part of this publication may be reproduced or trans-
mitted in any form by any means, electronic or mechanical, including print,
photocopy, recording, or any other information and retrieval system, without
prior consent of the publisher. Requests for permission to reprint or make
copies, and for any other information, should be addressed to the publisher:

George Braziller, Inc.
277 Broadway, Suite 708
New York, NY 10007

Library of Congress Cataloging-in-Publication Data
Villoro, Juan, 1956–
[Culpables. English]
The guilty: stories / by Juan Villoro; translated by Kimi Traube.—First edition.
        pages cm
ISBN 978-0-8076-0013-9
I. Traube, Kimi, translator. II. Title.
PQ7298.32.I55C8513 2015
863'.64–dc23

                2015004513

This publication was made possible with the encouragement of the Support
Program for Translation (PROTRAD) under Mexican cultural institutions.

Esta publicación fue realizada con el estímulo del Programa de Apoyo a la
Traducción (PROTRAD) dependiente de instituciones culturales mexicanas.

Designed by Rita Lascaro
Printed in the United States of America
First edition

CONTENTS

"He who holds back a word is its master;
he who utters it, its slave."
—KARL KRAUS

THE GUILTY

MARIACHI

"Should we do it?" asked Brenda.

I looked at her white hair, split into two silky blocks. I love young women with white hair. Brenda is 43 but her hair has been this way since she was 20. She likes to blame it on her first shoot. She was in the desert in Sonora, working as a production assistant, and she had to round up 400 tarantulas for some horror-movie genius. She pulled it off, but when she woke up the next morning she had white hair. I suppose it's genetic. Anyway, she likes to see herself as a heroine of professionalism who went gray because of tarantulas.

Strangely, albino women don't excite me. I don't want to explain my reasons because when they're made public I realize they aren't really reasons. I had enough of that with the horse thing. Nobody has ever seen me ride one. I am the only mariachi star who has never in his life mounted a horse. It took the reporters nineteen video clips to catch on. When they asked me about it, I answered, "I don't like transportation that shits." Very banal and very stupid. They published a photo of my platinum BMW and my 4x4 with the zebra skin seats. The Society for the Protection of Animals said they were ashamed of me. Plus, a reporter who hates me got his hands on a photo of me holding a high-powered rifle in Nairobi. I didn't hunt any lions because I didn't actually hit any, but there I was, all dressed up for safari. They accused me of being anti-Mexican for killing animals in Africa.

I made the horse declaration after singing until three a.m. in a rodeo arena at the San Marcos Festival. I was leaving for Irapuato two hours later. Do you know what it feels like to be fucked up and have to leave for Irapuato before the sun rises? I wanted to sink into a Jacuzzi, to stop being a mariachi. That's what I should have said: "I hate being a mariachi, singing under a five-pound hat, tearing myself to pieces, swollen with the resentment earned on ranches without electricity." Instead, I said something about horses.

They call me El Gallito de Jojutla, the Little Rooster from Jojutla, because that's where my father's from. They call me little rooster but I'm not an early riser. The trip to Irapuato was killing me—one of the many things that were killing me.

"Do you think I'm too sexy to have been a neurophysiologist?" Catalina asked me one night. I said yes to avoid an argument. She has the mind of a porno screenwriter:

she likes to imagine herself as a neurophysiologist, stirring up desires in the operating room. I didn't tell her that, but we made love with extra passion, as if to satisfy three curious onlookers. Afterwards I asked her to dye her hair white.

Since I met her, Cata's hair has been blue, pink, and cherry red. "Don't be a jackass," she answered. "There are no white dyes." That's when I understood why I like young women with white hair. They're not on the market. I told Cata this and she went back to talking like a porno screenwriter: "What's really going on here is that you want to fuck your mom."

Those words helped me a lot. They helped me leave my therapist. He thought the same thing as Cata. I had gone to see him because I was sick of being a mariachi. Before lying down on the couch, I'd made the mistake of looking at his chair: on the seat was an inflatable donut. Maybe it comforts some patients to know their doctor has hemorrhoids; someone intimate with suffering to help them confess their own horrors. But not me. I only stayed in therapy because my therapist was a fan. He knew all of my songs (the songs I sing: I haven't written any), and he thought it extremely interesting that I was there, with my famous voice, saying I'm fucking fed up with *ranchera* music.

Around the same time, an article appeared where they compared me to a bullfighter who'd gone through psychoanalysis to overcome his fear of the ring. They described his most terrible goring: his intestines fell out onto the sand in the Plaza Mexico. He picked them up and managed to run to the infirmary. That afternoon, he had been wearing dark purple and gold. Psychoanalysis helped him get back in the ring with that same suit on.

My doctor flattered me so ridiculously, I loved it. I could fill Azteca Stadium—including the field—and get 130, 000 souls to drool. The doctor drooled and I didn't even have to sing.

My mother died when I was two years old. This is an essential piece of information for understanding why I can cry on cue. All I have to do is think about a photo. I'm dressed in a sailor suit, she's hugging me and smiling at the man who would drive the Buick that flipped over. My father had drunk more than half a bottle of tequila at the *rancho* where they'd gone to eat lunch. I don't remember the funeral, but they say he threw himself weeping into the grave. He got me into *ranchera* songs. He also gave me the photo that makes me cry. My mother smiles, in love with the man who's taking her to a party. Outside the frame, my father snaps the shot with the bliss of the wretched.

It's obvious I want my mother back, but I *also* like women with white hair. I made the mistake of telling my therapist about the theory Cata got from the magazine *Contenido:* "You are Oedipal. That's why you don't like albino women, that's why you want a mommy with gray hair." The doctor asked me for more details about Cata. If there's one thing I can't fight her on, it's her notion that she's extremely sexy. This titillated the doctor and he stopped singing my praises. I went to our last session dressed as a mariachi because I was coming from a concert in Los Angeles. He asked to keep my tricolor bow tie. Does it make sense to talk about your inner life with a fan?

Catalina was also in therapy. This helped her to "internalize her sexiness." According to her, she could have been many things (almost all of them terrifying) because of her body. On the other hand, she believes the only thing I could have been is a mariachi. I have the voice, a face like an abandoned ranchero, and the eyes of a brave man who knows how to cry. Plus, I'm from here. Once I dreamed the reporters asked me, "Are you Mexican?" "Yes, but next time I won't be." This response, which in real life would have destroyed me, drove them wild in my dream.

My father made me record my first album at 16. I never went back to school or looked for another job. I was too successful for a career in industrial design.

I met Catalina the way I met my previous girlfriends: she told my agent she was available. Leo said Cata had blue hair and I figured she could probably dye it white. We started going out. I tried to convince her to bleach it, but she didn't want to. Plus, authentic white-haired women are inimitable.

The truth is I've found very few young women with white hair. I saw one in Paris, in a VIP lounge at the airport, but I froze up like an idiot. Then there was Rosa, who was 28 with beautiful white hair and a diamond-encrusted belly button which I only knew about because of the swimsuits she modeled. I fell for her so hard it didn't matter that she said "jillo" instead of "Jell-O." She didn't pay any attention to me. She hated *ranchera* music and wanted a blond boyfriend.

That's when I met Brenda. She was born in Guadalajara but lived in Spain. She went there to get away from mariachis. Now she was back in Mexico with a vengeance. Chus Ferrer, a genius filmmaker I knew nothing about, was in love with me and wanted me in his next movie, no matter the cost. Brenda had come to round me up.

She got chummy with Catalina and discovered they hated the same directors who had ruined their lives—Brenda's as a producer and Cata's as an eternally aspiring character actress.

"Brenda has a nice figure for her age, don't you think?" Cata said. "I'll take a look," I answered.

I had already looked. Catalina thought Brenda was past it. 'A nice figure' was her way of applauding an old nun for being thin.

I only like movies with spaceships and children who lose their parents. I didn't want to meet a gay genius who was in love with a mariachi who was, unfortunately, me. I read the screenplay so that Catalina would get off my fucking back. The truth is they only gave me bits and pieces, just the scenes in which I appeared. "Woody Allen does the same thing," Cata explained to me. "The actors only figure out what the movie is about when they see it in the theater. It's like life: you only see your own scenes and the big picture escapes you." That idea seemed so accurate I thought Brenda must have told it to her.

I suppose Catalina was hoping they would give her a role. "How are your scenes?" she said every three seconds. I read them at the worst possible time. My flight to El Salvador was cancelled because there was a hurricane, and I had to go by private jet. Amid the turbulence of Central America, the role seemed incredibly easy to me.

My character answered everything with "Heavy, man!" and let himself be adored by a gang of Catalonian bikers.

"What do you think about the scene with the kiss?" Catalina asked me. I didn't remember it. She explained that I was going to "tongue kiss" a "really filthy biker." She thought the idea was fantastic: "You're going to be the first mariachi without complexes, a symbol of the new Mexican." "The new Mexican kisses bikers?" I asked. Cata's eyes lit up: "Aren't you tired of being so typical? Chus's movie is going to catapult you to another audience. If you keep doing what you're doing, soon you'll only be interesting in Central America."

I didn't respond because at that moment a Formula 1 race was starting and I wanted to see Schumacher. Schumacher's life isn't like a Woody Allen script: he knows where the finish line is. When I was moved that Schumacher had donated a huge sum to the victims of the tsunami, Cata said: "Do you know why he's giving so much? He's ashamed of having gone there for sex tourism." There are moments like that. A man can accelerate up to 350 kilometers an hour, he can win and win and win, he can donate a fortune, and he can still be treated this way, in my own bed. I looked at the riding crop I go out on stage with (it's good for whacking away the flowers they throw at me). Then I made the mistake of picking up the crop and saying, "I forbid you to say that about my idol!" In one instant, Cata saw both my gay and my sadomasochistic potential: "So you have an idol now?" She smiled longingly, as if waiting for the first lash. "Fuck, yes," I said, and went down to the kitchen to make myself a sandwich.

That night I dreamed I was driving a Ferrari, running over sombreros until they were nice and flat, nice and flat.

My life was unraveling. My worst album, a series of *ranchera* songs composed by Alejandro Ramón, the hit maker from Sinaloa, had just gone platinum, and my concerts with the National Symphony at Bellas Artes had sold out. My face stretched out over four square meters on a billboard in the Alameda in Mexico City. I didn't care about any of it. I'm a star. Forgive me for saying it again. I don't want to complain, but I've never made a decision in my life. My father took charge of killing my mother, crying a lot, and making me into a mariachi. Everything else was automatic. Women seek me out through my agent. I fly a private jet when the commercial liners can't take off. Turbulence. That's what I depend on. What would I like? To float in the stratosphere, look down at Earth and see a blue bubble without a single sombrero.

I was thinking about that when Brenda called from Barcelona. I pictured her hair while she said, "Chus is flipping out over you. He put a hold on the house he's buying in Lanzarote while he waits for your answer. He wants you to grow your fingernails out like a vamp. Perfect for a slightly seedy queer. Do you mind being a vamp mariachi? You'd look just adorable. I fancy you, too. I suppose Cata's already told you." It excited me immensely that someone from Guadalajara could talk like that. I masturbated after I hung up, without even opening the copy of *Lord* magazine I keep in the bathroom. Later, when I was watching cartoons, I thought about the last part of our conversation. "I suppose Cata's already told you." What should she have told me? And why hadn't she?

Minutes later, Cata showed up to emphasize how great I'd be as a mariachi without prejudices (contradiction in terms: mariachis are a national prejudice). I didn't want to talk about that. I asked her what she'd discussed with Brenda.

"Everything. It's incredible how young she seems for her age. Nobody would ever think she's 43."

"What does she say about me?"

"I don't think you want to know."

"I don't care."

"She's been trying to convince Chus not to hire you. She thinks you're too naïve for a sophisticated role. She says that Chus has a chubby for you and she's been asking him not to think with his dick."

"That's what she's saying?"

"That's how the Spaniards talk!"

"Brenda is from Guadalajara!"

"She's been in Spain for decades, she defines herself as a fugitive from mariachis. Maybe that's why she doesn't like you."

I paused, then told her what had happened:

"Brenda called a little while ago. She said she's crazy about me."

Cata responded like a stony angel:

"I'm telling you she's super professional. She'll do anything for Chus."

I wanted to fight because I had just masturbated and didn't feel like making love. But I couldn't figure out how to offend her while she was unbuttoning her blouse. When she pulled off my pants, I thought about Schumacher, the master of mileage. That didn't excite me, I swear on my dead mother, but it filled me with will-power. We banged for three hours, not quite as long as a Formula 1 race. (Thanks to Brenda, I had started using the Spanish: "to bang.")

I finished off my concert at Bellas Artes with "*Se me olvidó otra vez.*" When I got to the line, "in the same city with the same people," I saw the journalist who hates me in the front row. Every year on my birthday, he publishes an article "proving" my homosexuality. His main argument is that I've made it to another birthday without getting married. A mariachi should breed like a stud bull. I thought about the biker I was supposed to tongue kiss. I looked at the journalist and felt assured he would be the only one to write that I'm a fag. Everyone else would talk about how virile it is to kiss another man just because the script calls for it.

The shoot was a nightmare. Chus Ferrer told me Fassbinder had made his star actress lick the floor of the set. He wasn't that much of a tyrant: he settled for smearing me with garbage to "muffle my ego." I had it easier than the lighting crew: he kept screaming "neo-fascist plebs!" at them. Whenever he could, he grabbed my ass.

I had to wait for so long on set that I became a Nintendo prodigy. I was also growing more and more attracted to Brenda. One night we went out to dinner on a terrace. Luckily, Catalina smoked some hash and fell asleep on her plate. Brenda told me she had had a "very tumultuous" life. Now she led a solitary existence; it was necessary to satisfy Chus Ferrer's production whims.

"You're the latest." She looked me in the eyes: "It took me so much work to convince you!"

"I'm not an actor, Brenda." I paused. "I don't want to be a mariachi, either," I added.

"What do you want?"

She smiled in an alluring way. I liked that she hadn't said: "What do you want *to be*?" It seemed to suggest: "What do you want *now*?" Brenda was smoking a small cigar. I looked at her white hair, sighed as only a mariachi who has filled stadiums can sigh, and said nothing.

One afternoon a porn star visited the set. "His penis is insured for a million euros," Catalina told me. Brenda was standing beside me. She said, "The long shot million," and explained that this had been the slogan for Mexico's National Lottery in the 70s. "You remember things from such a long time ago," Cata said. Even though the phrase was offensive, they went off happily to get dinner with the porn star. I stayed behind for the tongue kiss scene.

The actor who was playing the Catalonian biker was shorter than me and they had to put him on a stool. He had taken ginseng pills for the scene. Seeing as I had already conquered my prejudices, I thought it sounded like a faggy thing to do.

I was paid the same amount for four weeks of shooting as I got for one concert in any remote ranch in Mexico.

On the flight back they gave us tomato salad and Cata told me about a trick of the trade she'd heard from the porn star. He ate lots of tomatoes because it improved the taste of his semen. The female porn stars appreciated it. I was intrigued. Did that kind of courtesy really exist in porn? I ate the tomatoes off of my plate and hers, but when we got back to Mexico she said she was dead tired and didn't want to blow me.

The movie was called *Mariachi Baby Blues*. They invited me to the Madrid premier, and as I was walking the red carpet I saw a guy with his hands outstretched like he was measuring a yard. In Mexico that gesture would have been obscene. It was obscene in Spain too, but I only realized that after I saw the movie. There was a scene where the biker came close to touching my penis and a colossal member appeared onscreen, impressively erect. I thought that was why the porn star had visited the set. Brenda schooled me: "It's a prosthetic. Does it bother you that the public thinks it's yours?"

What does someone who has become an overnight genital phenomenon do? At the after-party, the queen of pink journalism gushed, "It's so shamelessly raunchy!" Brenda told me about celebrities who had been surprised on nude beaches and revealed penises like fire hoses. "But those penises are theirs!" I protested. She looked at me as if she was imagining the size of mine and seemed disappointed, but she was terribly nice and said nothing. I wanted to caress her hair, to cry into the crook of her neck. But then Catalina arrived, with glasses of champagne. I left the party early and walked through the streets of Madrid until the sun came up.

The sky had begun to yellow when I passed by the Parque del Retiro. A man was holding five very long leashes attached to five Huskies. He had cuts on his face and he was wearing cheap clothes. I would have given anything to have no obligations except walking rich people's dogs. The Huskies' blue eyes seemed mournful, as if the dogs wished I'd take them away with me and knew I couldn't.

I arrived at the Hotel Palace so tired I was barely surprised that Cata wasn't in the suite.

The next day, all of Madrid was talking about my raunchy shamelessness. I thought about killing myself but it seemed wrong to do it in Spain. I would mount a horse for the first time and blow my brains out in the Mexican countryside.

When I landed in Mexico City with still no word from Catalina, I discovered that the country adored me in a very strange way. Leo handed me a press folder full of praise for my foray into independent film. The words "manliness" and "virility" were repeated as often as "film in its pure state" and "total filmmaking." My take was that *Mariachi Baby Blues* was about a story inside a story inside a story, where at the end everybody was very content doing what they hadn't wanted to do at the beginning. A great achievement, according to the critics.

My next concert—in the Auditorio Nacional, no less—was tremendous. Everyone in the audience had a penis-shaped balloon. I had become the stallion of the fatherland. They started to call me the Gallito Inglés, the Cocky Little Rooster; one of my fan clubs changed its name to Club de Gallinas, The Hen Club.

Catalina had predicted the movie would make me a cult star. I tried finding her to remind her of that, but she was still in Spain. I got offers from everywhere to show up naked. My agent tripled his salary and invited me to see his new house, a mansion in the Pedregal neighborhood—twice as big as my own. A priest was there. He held a mass to bless the house and Leo thanked God for putting me at his side. Then he asked me to go with him to the garden. He told me the actress Vanessa Obregón wanted to meet me.

Leo's ambition knows no limits. It was in his own best interest for me to date the bombshell of *banda* music. But I could no longer be with a woman without disappointing her or having to explain the absurd situation the movie had created.

I gave thousands of interviews but no one believed I wasn't proud of my penis. I was declared Sexiest Latino by a magazine in Los Angeles, Sexiest Bisexual by a magazine in Amsterdam, and Most Unexpected Sexpot by a magazine in New York. But I couldn't take my pants off without feeling diminished.

Finally Catalina came back from Spain to humiliate me with her new life: she had become the porn star's girlfriend. She told me this in a restaurant where I demonstrated the poor taste of ordering a tomato salad. I thought about the porn king's diet, but I barely had time to distract myself with that irritation because Cata was asking me for a fortune in palimony. I gave it to her so that she wouldn't talk about my penis.

I went to see Leo at two in the morning. He took me to the room he calls his "study" just because there is an encyclopedia in there. He ran his bare feet back and forth over a puma skin rug while I talked. He was wearing a robe with dragons on it, like an actor playing a lurid spy. I told him about Cata's extortion.

"Think of it as an investment," he told me.

That calmed me down a little, but I felt drained. When I got home, I couldn't masturbate. A plumber had made off with my copy of *Lord* magazine and I didn't even miss it.

Leo kept pulling strings. The limo that arrived to take me to the MTV Latino gala had first picked up a spectacular mulatta who was smiling in the back seat. Leo had hired her to accompany me to the ceremony and increase my sexual legend. I liked talking to her—she knew all about the guerrillas in El Salvador—but I didn't try anything because she was looking at me with measuring-tape eyes.

I went back to therapy. I explained that Catalina was happy because of an actual big dick and I was unhappy because of an imaginary one. Could life be that basic? The doctor said this happened to 90 percent of his patients. I quit therapy because I didn't want to be such a cliché.

My fame is too strong a drug. I need what I hate. I toured everywhere, threw sombreros into grandstands, got down on my knees and sang *"El hijo desobediente."* I recorded an album with a hip-hop group. One afternoon, in the main square of Oaxaca, I sat down on a pigskin chair and listened to marimba music for a long while. I drank two glasses of mezcal, nobody recognized me, and I believed that I was happy. I looked at the blue sky and the white line left by a plane. I thought about Brenda and dialed her on my cell.

"It took you long enough," was the first thing she said. Why hadn't I looked for her sooner? With her, I didn't have to pretend. I asked her to come see me. "I have a life, Julián," she said in an exasperated voice. But she pronounced my name like it was a word I had never heard before. She wasn't going to drop anything for me. I canceled my Bajío tour.

I spent three terrifying days in Barcelona without being able to see her. Brenda was "tied up" in a shoot. We finally saw each other, in a restaurant that seemed to be designed for Japanese denizens of the future.

"You want to know if I know you?" she said, and I thought she was quoting a *ranchera* song. I laughed, just to react, and then she looked me in the eyes. She told me she knew the date of my mother's death, the name of my ex-therapist, my desire to be in orbit. She had admired me since a time she called "immemorial." It had all started when she saw me sweat on Telemundo. It took her an incredible amount of work to get together with me. She had convinced Chus to hire me, wrote my parts into the screenplay, introduced Cata to the porn star, planned the scene with the artificial penis to shake up my whole life. "I know who you are, and my hair is white," she smiled. "Maybe you think I'm manipulative. I'm a producer, which is almost the same thing: I produced our meeting."

I looked her in the eyes, red from sleepless nights on film shoots. I acted like a stupid mariachi and said, "I'm a stupid mariachi." "I know." Brenda caressed my hand.

Then she told me why she wanted me. Her story was horrible. She explained why she hated Guadalajara, mariachis, tequila, tradition, custom. I promised not to tell anyone. I can only say that she lived to escape that story, until she understood that escaping it was the only story she had. I was her return ticket.

I thought we would sleep together that night but she still had one more production:

"I don't mean to tell you how to do your job, but you have to clear up the penis thing."

"The penis thing isn't my job: you all invented it!"

"Exactly, we invented it. A European cinematic trick. I had forgotten what a penis can do in Mexico. I don't want to go out with a man stuck onto a penis."

"I'm not stuck onto a penis, mine's sort of little," I said.

"How little?"

Brenda was interested.

"Normal little. See for yourself."

But she wanted me to understand her moral principles.

"Your fans have to see it," she answered. "Be brave enough to be normal."

"I'm not normal: I'm the Gallito de Jojutla, even pharmacies sell my albums!"

"You have to do it. I'm sick of this phallocentric world."

"But are *you* going to want *my* penis?"

"Your normal sort of little sort of penis?"

Brenda dropped her hand to my crotch, but she didn't touch me.

"What do you want me to do?" I asked.

She had a plan. She always has a plan. I would appear in another movie, a ferocious criticism of the celebrity world, and I would do a full frontal. My audience would have a stark, authentic version of me. When I asked who would direct the movie, I got another surprise. "Me," answered Brenda. "The film is called *Guadalajara*".

She didn't give me the whole screenplay, either. The scenes I appeared in were weird, but that didn't mean anything. The kind of films I think are weird win prizes. One afternoon, during a break in shooting, I went into her trailer and asked, "What do you think will happen to me after *Guadalajara*?" "Do you really care?" she responded.

Brenda had tried harder than anybody else to be with me. Had I embraced her in that moment I would have burst into tears. I was afraid of seeming weak when I touched her but I was more afraid that she might never want to touch me. I had learned one thing from Cata, at least: there are parts of the body that can't be platonic.

"Are you going to sleep with me?" I asked her.

"We have one scene left," she said, caressing her own hair.

She cleared the set to film me naked. Everyone else left in a bad mood because the caterers had just arrived with the food. Brenda put me next to a table surrounded by an enticing scent of cold cuts.

She stood in front of me for a moment. She looked at me in a way I'll never forget, as if we were about to cross a river. She smiled, and said what we were both waiting for:

"Should we do it?"

She got behind the camera.

On the buffet table, there was a plate of salad. I was a foot away from it.

Life is chaos but it has its signals: before I took off my pants, I ate a tomato.

HOLDING PATTERN

I'm so discouraged by reality that to me, airplanes seem cozy. I resign myself to movies I don't want to see and food I don't want to taste, like I'm practicing a spiritual discipline. A samurai with headphones and a plastic knife. Suspended, cell phone off, enjoying a Nirvana where there's nothing to decide. That's what air travel is—a way of delaying the numbers trying to catch up with me.

The last call I got on land was from Clara. I was in the Barcelona airport. Anguished, she asked me, "Do you think she'll come back?" She was talking about our cat, Única. Her name means *only one*. "Has there been an earthquake?" I asked. Cats can sense earthquakes. Something—a vibration in the air—lets them know the earth is going to split open. Time to head outdoors.

Male cats are the anticipatory seismologists. Female cats stay at home, especially Angoras. That's what we'd been told. Still, Única had run away twice, no earthquakes required.

"Maybe she's picking up on emotional earthquakes," Clara joked on the phone. Then she mentioned that the Rendóns had invited her up to Valle de Bravo. If my flight didn't get in on time, she'd go on her own. She was yearning for a weekend of sailboats and sun.

"Will you ever take a direct flight?" she asked before saying goodbye.

I live a zigzag life. For some reason, my itineraries all lead to cities that require connections: Antwerp, Oslo, Barcelona. I work for a company that produces the best tasteless water in the world. It's not a disparaging phrase. People don't drink our water for the taste, they drink it because it weighs less in your mouth. The luxury of lightness. The planet is always thirsty. Everyone needs to drink. But some demand the additional delight of insubstantial water.

I travel frequently to places that purchase expensive water, and jet lag is my constant condition. I've gotten used to the discrepancy in perception, the things I see when I should be sleeping. I read a lot in the long hours on flights, or I think, with my face against the plane's oval window. I often come up with ideas that seem mystical and then evaporate like hand lotion when I land.

Our departure from Barcelona was delayed. Now we're flying over London, off schedule. "We're in a holding pattern," the pilot says. There is no room for us.

The plane leans into a leisurely curve. We'll circle like fruit flies until a runway opens up. The lovely autumn light makes the lawns below us shine, with the Thames sparkling like the blade of a sword and the city scattering toward inconceivable limits.

London is an hour behind Barcelona. Those minutes that haven't happened yet are an advantage for making a connection, but I don't want to think about them. I'll have to take the bus from Terminal 2 to Terminal 4, like joining the delirium of a theme park. I think about O.J. Simpson before the murder accusation, back when he shone as a desperate success known to devour yards on the football field and in ads where he was about to miss a plane. I like that about airports. They only have internal tension. Everything exterior is erased. You have to run in pursuit of a gate. That's it. Your destination is called "Gate 6." O.J. was made for that, to run far away from intercepted phone calls, broken love, empty glances, bloodied clothes.

The captain's voice has been replaced by landing music. Techno-flamenco. We circle, miles above the ground, all of us watching the clock. How many flights will be missed on this flight? If the music were different we wouldn't worry as much. In some distant office, someone decided it was good to land to the beat of astral gypsies. And maybe it is. The discord of modernity and oranges. Music meant for arriving, not for waiting indefinitely with gates closing below.

I've missed enough connections for Clara to suspect it's part of a plan. "That much bad luck isn't normal." Frankfurt shut down by snow, Barajas by strike. I've had to sleep in hotels where you feel like you're wasting an opportunity to kill yourself. You move from the attractive provisional order of the airport to the sordidness of transitory objects. A rented bed somewhere no one expects to see you again.

Clara's only partially right. My bad luck isn't normal, but it's also not that bad. Once I missed a plane at Heathrow under a rosy sky. The arranged hotel turned out to be nice. In the distance, jumbo jets moved along the runways like the shadows of whales, and in the lobby I ran into Nancy. She had missed her flight, too. We work in far off cities for the same company.

We had dinner at a pub where they'd turned on a Chelsea soccer game. Neither of us likes soccer but we watched the game with strange intensity. We were living borrowed hours. Nancy has incredible blonde hair; it looks like she washes it with the water we sell. I've always liked her, but only then, in that time outside of time, did it seem logical to take her hand and play with her wedding ring.

She left my room at dawn. I saw her silhouette in the cold light of the street. In the distance, a triangle of purple lights marked the juncture of the two avenues that led to the airport. The control towers looked like lighthouses gone adrift, radar sets spinning in search of signals. I breathed in Nancy's perfume on my hand and understood, for once, the artificial beauty of the world.

We saw each other again, at meetings and conventions, without alluding to our missed-flight encounter. When Clara suggested I was getting delayed on purpose, I remembered that singular episode and my tone of voice incriminated me, like O.J. before the jury, when he put on the black glove worn by his wife's murderer and it fit perfectly. I wanted to run but I wasn't in an airport.

"Is there someone else?" Clara asked me. I said no, and it was true, but she looked at me like I was a TV snowing ashes.

Now I'm flying over Heathrow again. What are the chances Nancy's missing a flight, too? If we saw each other, could we be indifferent to our geometry?

Nancy didn't imply a repeat encounter was possible. Still, I couldn't help noticing her ambivalence when she said, "You know where you're taking off from, but not which sky you're going to." Then she laid her head on my chest.

I page through the airline magazine. Enviable land-scapes, the face of a famous architect, and what I least expected: a short story by Elías Rubio. Even though he's publishing more frequently, finding him is always an unpleasant surprise. Elías almost married Clara. His style is striking—to anyone not married to her. I can't read a single paragraph without feeling like he's sending her messages.

The techno-flamenco hurts my ears. There isn't much time left to make my connection, and I start looking for excuses to explain to Clara that I didn't miss the plane on purpose. I need some other problem. That's why I read the story. Elías is a leech who feeds on reality. He's one of the reasons I'm sick of it.

The first time Única ran away, we hung posters on tele-phone poles; we left our number at the local vet; we went on a radio program that specialized in runaway pets.

Female cats don't leave but ours had gone. One afternoon, Clara asked me again if I really didn't care that
she couldn't get pregnant. She had been drinking some
tea from India and her words smelled like cloves. I told
her I didn't, and I thought about the cat's absurd name,
the one Clara had picked as a heroic wisecrack, the one
that had transformed over time into a painful irony. I
looked away. When I looked back, Clara was watching
something in the garden. It was getting dark. Behind a
bush, there was an opaque, hazy glow. Clara squeezed
my hand. Seconds later, we saw Única's fur, soiled during
her absence.

That night, Clara caressed me as if her hands were
made from a rain that leaves things dry. At least, that's
how Elías described the scene, which he had used uned-
ited in his story. The title was loathsome: "The Included
Third." Was he referring to himself? Was he still seeing
Clara? Did she tell him those kind of minutiae? The
repugnant writer accurately observed a nervous gesture
of hers, the way she winds her hair around her hand.
Clara only releases it once she's made some inscrutable
decision.

As I read further, my spine freezes: Elías had foreseen
the cat's second disappearance. After reconciling with
her husband—a piddling talc salesman—the heroine
realizes happiness is nothing but suffering held in place.
The cat's return had completed a picture. Everything
was in order, but real life demanded a change, a fissure.
The woman lifted a hand to her hair, wound the strands
around it, and let them go. Without a word, she picked
up the cat and took it to the countryside.

Had that really happened? Had Clara gotten rid of the cat so she could blame it on my absences, or to prepare for her own absence? Elías was full of vengeful fantasies (not for nothing was he a writer!), but the story's content wasn't imaginary. Too much of it had actually happened. What was Única's meaning in the story? Was Clara freeing herself when she freed the cat? When Clara had called me in Barcelona, she talked around the cat like a clue. Only now, suspended in the London air, did I realize it.

Holding pattern: if I don't get there on time, she'll spend the weekend with the Rendóns, the couple that at some hazy point in the past introduced her to Elías Rubio.

A grinding of metal: the landing gear. I can still make my flight. Terminal 4, Gate 6.

Is Clara starting to sense my missed flights the way cats sense earthquakes? What does she miss when she misses Única? What time is it in my country? Is she winding her hair around her hand? Will she release it before I get to my gate? Will there be a rosy sunset in Heathrow? Is someone else missing a flight? Is our plane displacing another which could still arrive on time?

The turbines give a deafening roar. We touch down. My body feels numb, conscious of passing into a different logic.

What happens on the ground. The geometry of the sky.

THE WHISTLE

"Ghosts come out of nowhere, but the dead just come back." That's what Lupillo said to me as he squeezed out a sponge. You have to believe massage therapists. They're the only ones on a team who'll tell you the truth, the only ones whose sole aspiration is to spray on the analgesic.

Lupillo's line was the first sign I'd become an outcast. The second was that nobody played any welcome-back tricks on me. I had returned to Estrella Azul, the team where I got my start. If anyone had still cared about me, they would have pissed in my shampoo. That's how simple the world of soccer is.

"We even held a funeral mass for you!" added Lupillo. I was watching his bald head, shiny as a crystal ball. Yes, they'd held a mass for me where the priest praised my hustle and integrity, virtues death had conferred. Dead men have integrity.

I almost died with the Mexicali Toucans. I've seen pictures of people playing soccer in minefields. In any war there are desperate people, desperate enough not to care about losing a foot, as long as they can shoot a ball. Maybe if I went to war I'd think there was nothing more badass than kicking something round, like your enemy's head. In my heaven, there are no soccer balls. Heaven for strikers is full of them, I guess. But for defensive midfielders, heaven is an empty field where there's nothing to do and you can finally scratch your nuts, the balls you haven't been able to touch your whole career.

I almost died with the Mexicali Toucans. I'm saying it again because it's absurd and I still don't understand it. I wonder if the bomb was ball-shaped, if it was like the one The Road Runner hands to Wile E. Coyote in the cartoons. A stupid thing to worry about, but I can't stop.

I spent three days under rubble. They figured I was dead. I was erased from every team's roster. (Not that many clubs were fighting over me, but I like to think I had to be erased.)

When I woke up, the Toucans had sold their franchise. When the bomb exploded, so did the dream of having a team that close to the United States, on the only field below sea level. There were lots of rumors when the news got out. Almost all of them had to do with narcotrafficking: the Gulf cartel didn't want the Pacific cartel hijacking its move into soccer.

I didn't know anything about Mexicali until the triplets walked into my room in Mexico City. I'd fractured my ankle and was sick of watching TV.

"Somebody's here for you," said Tere. From her expression, I should have known my three visitors had buzz cuts.

Not just that: they were enormously fat, like sumo wrestlers. Colored tattoos spilled out from under their t-shirts. All three had neatly trimmed goatees.

They set a case of Tecate beer on the bed, as if it was some incredible gift.

"The brewery's close to the stadium."

That was what they said.

I've always liked Tecate beer. Maybe what I like most is the red can with the shield. Still, it wasn't a great way to start a conversation.

The fat men were weird. Maybe they were insane. They were the board of directors for the Mexicali Toucans, and the brewery was their sponsor.

I asked them their names and they answered like a hip-hop group:

"Triplet A," "Triplet B," "Triplet C."

Could I do business with people like this?

"We like to keep a low profile," whichever one of them said. "No photos, no box seats, no names. We love soccer."

"Sorry, but where the fuck is Mexicali?" I asked.

They explained things I've never forgotten that possibly weren't true. In Porfirio Díaz's day, the Mexicali desert was famous for a platoon of soldiers that disappeared there. They lost their way and all of them died, fried to a crisp. No one could live in that desert. Until the Chinese arrived. They were allowed to stay because everyone was sure they would die. Who could survive 120° heat below sea level? The Chinese.

As they talked, I started to distinguish between them in a strange way. They appeared to have Chinese blood and I could only tell them apart the way most Mexicans differentiate tattooed Chinese people—the one with the dragon, the one with the knife, the one with the bleeding heart.

"Do you like Peking duck?" asked Triplet C.

Then they started talking about money. They mentioned a number and my throat seized up.

I didn't answer. The triplets were barely thirty years old. Their obesity made them look like radioactive babies from some Chinese sci-fi flick.

"That's what you're worth." Triplet B scratched his beard. "The Toucans really need you."

"The brewery is backing us." They gestured to the case on the bed.

At that point, I should have understood they were planning to launder their money with beer. Narcos are so powerful, they're free to act like narcos. They didn't need to dress as geography teachers.

Instead of asking for a few days to consider, I asked the question that would be my undoing:

"Are you thinking of hiring any Argentinians?"

"No fucking way!" said Triplet A.

He smiled, and I thought I saw the gleam of a diamond on his incisor.

I had just turned 33, and I had a fractured ankle. I couldn't afford to turn down this season in the desert. In the match where I broke my bone, I'd scored an own goal. "The Last Sensation of Christ," wrote some snarky reporter, rejoicing in my martyrdom.

"You're playing with fire," Tere told me. I liked that. I liked playing with fire.

She saw things differently. Anyone who was interested in me had to be suspect.

"There are no toucans in Mexicali."

She kept saying that, day after day, until we stopped talking about toucans and started talking about Argentinians.

I owe Maradona's country two fractures, sixteen red cards, and one season on the bench, thanks to a coach who accused me of "prioritizing my trauma." What I didn't know was I would owe my divorce to the Argentinians, too.

Baldy Díaz played on two teams with me. One of those guys whose head was fat with talk; in interviews, he spoke like he'd just come from breakfast with God.

He had a big mouth, but nothing on him was as big as his cock. You can't avoid seeing things like that in the locker room. None of this would've been important, except Tere knew about it too. About Baldy's size, I mean. The time she accused me of "playing with fire," she had just come back from visiting him. Later, I found them in my own bed. It wasn't the classic situation where the husband arrives home early. "I'll be home at six," I told Tere, and at six I found her riding Baldy's giant cock. It was her way of telling me she didn't want to go to Mexicali.

We got divorced through the mail, thanks to a lawyer with five gold rings whom the triplets found for me.

On the way to Mexicali, I went through La Rumorosa, a mountain pass where the wind blows so hard it flips trucks. Looking down from the cliffs, I could see the remains of crashed cars at the bottom. I felt a weird kind of peace. A place for things to end. A place to end my career.

I continued as midfielder, but acted more like a fifth defender. I recovered balls at a reasonable rate for the triplets, although more often, I was being recovered from between the opposing team's legs.

I got used to playing through the pain. Then I got used to the injections. I played on painkillers more often than a normal body should. But my body isn't normal. It's a kicked-in lump. When she was feeling for my nerve with the needle, the doctor talked about my calcified flesh, as if I were turning into a wall. I liked that idea: a wall the opposing team smashes into, a wall on which Argentinians crack open their heads.

One of the triplets had a white tiger. Feeding it cost more than my salary. I got on the triplet's good side when I asked him to pay me the same as his pet.

"I have an orca, too," he told me. "Which would you rather have, a tiger salary or an orca salary?" He narrowed his mysterious Chinese eyes.

I know nothing about animals. My salary went up, but I never knew which animal it corresponded to.

I liked Mexicali, especially the food. Peking duck, wontons, sweet and sour pork ribs. That's the traditional food around there. In one of the restaurants, I met Lola. She was working as a waitress. Her parents were Chinese, and she pronounced her name "Lo-l-a." I liked to sit in front of the electric waterfall painting. I'd watch it until they pulled out the plug. Lola told me a Chinese guy had been hypnotized once, watching the painting. He only woke up when they put a phone playing "Yellow River" to his ear.

"Have you ever heard that song?" Lola asked me.

I told her I hadn't.

"Fancy music, Yangtze music." Sometimes she'd talk like that. You didn't know if she was saying two different things, or if the words that came after cancelled out the ones she'd said before.

The hypnotized Chinese guy had worked for the triplets.

"Don't believe what people say about them," explained Lola. "They're not from the Pacific cartel. They work for the other Pacific. Their mafia is from Taiwan." She said the last part as if it was a really good thing.

After meals, Lola would hand out toys. Little plastic cats with light-up bellies, things like that. They all fell apart ten minutes later.

"The triplets bring the toys," she told me as I walked out with something broken in my hands. It was very presumptuous of me to think they'd bought my contract with drugs. They'd paid for me with toys that fell apart.

The triplets promised that the Toucans would have no Argentinian players, but one of them took a trip to La Pampa anyway. He came back with a tattoo of Che Guevara. Some people said the wind in Patagonia drove him nuts. Others said he got high on a boat headed to a glacier, fell into the icy water, and was pulled out frozen stiff. Now he wanted everyone to call him Triplet Che.

Part of his craziness was good for the team. He had hired a very rare kind of player for the Toucans, one with more of a future than a past. Patricio Banfield had just turned 22 and was coming from Rosario Central. He kicked the ball like he was advertising shoes. "You gift-wrap yourself," the trainer told me when Patricio proved he could punt me all over the field.

The only weird thing about Patricio was the way he'd whistle to catch your attention. "It's a habit from the *pueblo*," he'd say. "I like everyone to know where I am." I got used to recovering balls and hearing his whistle, way off in the distance. I'd shoot hard in that direction. We didn't perform any miracles, but Patricio scored consistently. A long-suffering ace, trying to shine in a place that only existed because the Chinese had survived the sun.

I don't like animals, but I was tired of coming home to a silent house, so I bought a parrot. It talked as much as an Argentinian. I offered it to Lola, but she told me, "Parrots bring bad luck." That was the first sign of what was going to happen. Or maybe not. Maybe the first sign was how good I felt in La Rumorosa, staring at the cars that had gone over the edge. "In soccer, the end comes soon enough," Lupillo had told me when I was just starting. "That's not the problem. The problem is it never stops ending. Memories last a lot longer than legs: you'd better make them good." I was in the desert, ending a career of bad memories, but I wasn't sad to be there. A place to make my exit, for everything to end and nothing to matter.

I even got used to the parrot. I'd sit with it on the porch of the house. A one-story house with screens in the windows. Across the street, there was a trailer home where a gringo couple lived. For forty years, the husband had sold caramels at Woolworth's; his pension went further in Mexico. The only way he was going back to the other side was in a coffin. My parrot was going to outlive my neighbors. But none of that upset me. Now it seems sad, but out there I only thought about the sun. How to stop it beating down on me so hard.

One afternoon, I broke open a fortune cookie in Lola's restaurant. It said, "Follow your star." Just that.

That afternoon, one of the triplets came out of the restaurant's kitchen, followed by a cloud of steam. He looked at the fortune cookie and made a prediction: "You'll go back to Estrella Azul." Then he walked out of the restaurant very slowly, as if we were hallucinating his movements: a fat, floating ghost. Going back to Estrella Azul seemed like a terrible idea. Maybe that's why I thought following my star meant being with Lola. I looked at her young, Chinese face; not pretty or ugly, just young and Chinese. She smelled like tea. I proposed we see each other some place else. She didn't want to. "Your parrot brings bad luck," she repeated, as if the animal was part of my body, or we were trapped in a legend, and the parrot housed the spirit of her dead Chinese grandfather.

Together with my change, she gave me a little bag with a Chinese character on it.

"It means 'lots of wind,'" she explained.

I thought about La Rumorosa and this time those crashed cars made me anxious. I remained nervous until Lola turned off the waterfall. I didn't want to go back there.

I broke up with Lola despite never having been with her. Though, I had liked the team cheerleaders long before that. When I saw them for the first time, I felt as if I had selected each one, but I focused mostly on Nati.

Patricio Banfield paved the way for me and Nati. His girlfriend—a country singer who sang with too much feeling, making *Star Wars* faces—was Nati's friend. We started going out, and one morning Nati forgot her little cheerleader shorts at my house. She left them in the kitchenette, next to her bowl of cereal. I looked at the gringos' trailer through the window, at the parrot's cage, the honey-colored light of the desert. I finished what Nati had left in the bowl; the best thing I've ever eaten.

Another day, while we watched the blood-colored dawn, she told me they were going to sell the whole team. I asked her how she knew. She didn't answer and I looked her straight in the eye. On the field, there's nothing worse than looking into the eyes of someone from the opposing team. He can insult and spit on you all match without rousing you, but look directly at him, and your blood starts to boil. That's what happened to Zidane in Germany. I'm sure of it. The fury in his eyes. They've red-carded me for trying to see what my rivals store in there. With Nati, it was different. Her eyes said nothing. Two still coins. I hated being unable to agitate her. She said,

"Patricio should stay. If he does, they won't sell the franchise."

My friend Patricio was in negotiations with Toltecas, a strong team out of Mexico City that never wins the leagues but goes far enough to buy and sell players. Here, business isn't about being champions, it's about making trades.

One day there was no hot water in the locker room, and they told us the triplets were broke. On a different day, they told us the Chinese liked football and wanted to buy the team. Another day they told us the triplets' enemies didn't like that the Chinese liked football. Patricio talked with promoters all day long.

One night we went to the Nefertiti to dance, with Patricio and the country singer. I remember it better than my debut in the Premier League. A sarcophagus appeared in the middle of the dance floor, and out of it came a spectacular woman, completely naked. She floated over to Patricio, who was drinking Diet Coke, and pulled him up to dance. I stared intently at the hieroglyphics tattooed on her back, as if I could decipher them. That's what I was doing when the bomb exploded.

Hours later I opened my eyes and saw a bracelet shaped like a little snake. The woman who'd danced with Patricio had been wearing it. I smelled chemicals. There was a bottle of water near me. I drank desperately, like I do at the end of a match. I tried to move, but pain shot through my right leg. Then I heard a whistle.

I learned from the papers that I was rescued two days after the explosion. I spent a week in the hospital. Nati didn't visit me. One of her friends told me she'd found a job in Las Vegas.

Maybe Patricio had been the target of the bomb, the crack midfielder showing off and tempted by other teams. Did the triplets need a martyr, or was it someone else trying to fuck them over? The only certain thing was that Patricio had made it out of the explosion unharmed.

While I was in rehab rolling a bottle under my foot, he had started to shine with Toltecas.

The Toucans were sold and my contract was auctioned off for a piddling amount. When Estrella Azul bought me, the papers called it "A Sentimental Recruit." In the locker room, though, nobody knew I was back because of sentimentality. Here was the star my fortune cookie had promised.

That's when Lupillo said that ghosts come out of nowhere and the dead just come back. I'd gone to Mexicali to find the end, but as the sportscasters put it, "It's not over till it's over." When can something with no finish line ever come to an end?

I missed the waterfall that never stopped falling. I missed having a crazy board of directors that paid me the same wage as a tiger. I missed the desert where it didn't matter that there was nobody around to see me. I missed Nati's hands after they folded something very precisely, then touched my calcified flesh and I felt them, gentle and cold. The best thing about Nati was that I never knew why she was with me. It could have been a horrendous reason, but she never told me what it was.

It took me a while to get back into the rhythm of things. I went to a doctor's office opposite Gate 6 of Estrella Stadium. I became a fan of electric massages, and then I became a fan of Marta, a dark-skinned girl who touched me with the tips of her fingers more than was strictly necessary, barely grazing me with her long nails. The first time I made love to her, she confessed she was in love with Patricio. That detail had stopped surprising me. Sooner or later, they all asked: "Did he really save your life?"

Yes, Patricio had saved me. He had searched for me in the ruins of the Nefertiti alongside the firefighters, while in Mexico City they were already performing my funeral mass. He was still Argentinian, but even my parrot missed him.

Around that time, people were talking about the triplets. How they were killed with dynamite. They had only identified one, by his Che tattoo. But the other two had also been there. The police knew this because they'd counted the teeth in the rubble. The triplets died next to a warehouse full of contraband Chinese toys.

I remember the day they came to visit me with the case of beer. "We rise like foam," they'd told me. They were younger than me. Their bodies had swollen up as if they knew they wouldn't live very long. All three of them, as if they had made a pact to inflate together.

Against every prediction, Estrella Azul made it to the finals against Toltecas. Patricio called to wish me luck. Then, casually, he added:

"The board of directors needs new recruits. They put a price on my contract."

Every three or four years, Toltecas overhauls their roster. No other team makes as much in commissions. People like the triplets blow up. People like us get traded.

The first leg ended in a dirty o-o. Patricio was kicked viciously. The referee turned out to be my parrot's vet. He hated Argentinians. He didn't call the fouls made on my friend. Even I gave Patricio a few extra kicks.

I don't know what that second leg looked like from the outside. I never saw it on TV. For me, that afternoon marked the end of soccer, though movement remained an unending agony. We were o-o at minute 88. You could smell the disappointment of a final gone to penalties. Patricio had played like a ghost. We'd kicked him too much in the first match.

Suddenly, I swept the ball away and kept it. It was as if everything was spinning and the sun was beating down from inside me. There was a shattering silence, like when I woke half dead in the Nefertiti. I looked up, not at the field, but at the sky. Then I saw the grass all around me; an island, the very last island. It was like breaking open a fortune cookie. Everything stopped: the water in the electric waterfall, the sweat on the triplets' cheeks, Nati's hands on my back, the twelve teams who'd kicked me, the red, white and green jersey I never got to wear, the needle feeling for my nerves. And then I saw nothing, just the desert, the only place I could make a backwards play.

I heard a whistle. Patricio was open on the forward line. I saw his jersey, an enemy to both of us. I passed him the ball.

He was alone in front of the goalie, but simply scoring wasn't enough for him. He launched a beautiful little curve shot that caressed the ball towards the corner. I admired this, the play I'd never been capable of making, which was now just as much mine as the jeers and insults and cups of beer they threw at me, and which finally meant something different.

I walked off the field and started my life.

THE GUILTY

The shears lay on the table. They were enormous. My father had used them to butcher chickens. Since his death, Jorge has carried the shears with him everywhere. Maybe it's normal for a psychopath to sleep with a gun under his pillow. My brother isn't a psychopath. He isn't normal, either.

I found him in the bedroom, doubled over, struggling to pull off his T-shirt. It was 108 degrees. Jorge was wearing a shirt made of coarse cloth, the kind that sticks to you like a second skin.

"Open it up!" he shouted, his head swaddled in fabric. He gestured vaguely to the weakest point in the weave; a part I had no trouble finding.

I got the shears and cut his shirt. I eyed the tattoo on his back. It annoyed me that the shears were good for something. Jorge made senseless things useful; for him, that's what having talent meant.

He embraced me as if being anointed with his sweat was some kind of baptism. Then he looked at me with eyes sunken by drugs, suffering, too many movies. He had energy to spare, an inconvenient thing on a summer afternoon on the outskirts of Sacramento. His last visit, Jorge had kicked the fan and broken off one of its blades. Now the machine made a noise like a baby's rattle and barely nudged the air. Not one of us six brothers thought about replacing it. The farm was being sold. It still smelled like birds; white feathers still hung on the barbed wire.

I had proposed a different place for us to meet, but Jorge needed something he called "accordance." We had all lived there once, crammed in. We read the Bible at meals, scaled the roof to watch shooting stars. We were beaten with the rake used to scrape up chicken shit, dreamed about running away and returning to burn the house down.

"Come with me." Jorge went out to the porch. He had arrived in a Windstar minivan, a real luxury for him.

He pulled two buckled cases out of the van. He was so thin that in the absurd immensity of the desert, it looked like he was holding scuba tanks. They were typewriters.

He put them at opposite ends of the dining room table and assigned me the one with the stuck ñ-key. For weeks, we would sit face to face. Jorge imagined himself a screenwriter. He had a contact in Tucson, which isn't exactly the Mecca of cinema, a gringo who was interested in a "raw story" that apparently we could tell. The

Windstar and a two-thousand-dollar advance were proof of his interest.

The gringo believed in Mexican cinema as in a quintessential guacamole. There was too much hatred and passion at the border not to exploit it on-screen. In Arizona, farmers shot at migrants lost on their land ("a hot safari," the man had said; Jorge made him sound like an evangelist). Then, the unlikely producer had mixed a red margarita. "Mexican essence," he said, "rests among a pile of corpses."

The gringo's greatest extravagance was trusting my brother. Jorge's filmmaker training consisted of driving American drug addicts around the Oaxaca coasts. They told him about movies we had never seen in Sacramento. When he moved to Torreón, he would go to the video store every day just because it had air conditioning. They hired him to make his presence seem normal and because he could recommend movies he'd never seen.

My brother came back to Sacramento with a strange look in his eyes. I was sure it had something to do with Lucía. She had been so bored out here, in this wasteland, that when Jorge returned she gave him a chance. Even back then, when he was still a reasonable weight and had all his teeth, my brother looked like a cosmic nutjob, like someone who'd been abducted by a UFO. Maybe he had the pedigree of a man who's gone great distances; the point is Lucia let him into her house behind the gas station. It was hard to believe someone with Lucía's body and her obsidian eyes couldn't find a better candidate among the truckers who stopped to pump diesel. Jorge took the luxury of leaving her, as well.

He didn't want to tie himself to Sacramento. But he wore it on his skin: he had shooting stars tattooed on his back, the "Tears of San Fortino" that fall each year on August 12th. It was an incredible spectacle we watched as children. Plus, his middle name is Fortino.

My brother was made for leaving, but also for coming back. He arranged his most recent return by phone. He said our broken lives looked like those of other filmmakers. Latin artists were making it big. The man in Tucson believed in fresh talent. Curiously, the "raw story" was mine; that's why I had a typewriter in front of me.

I had also made it out of Sacramento. For years, I drove semis on both sides of the border. In the shifting landscapes of that period, my only constant was Tecate beer. I joined Alcoholics Anonymous after flipping a truck full of fertilizer in Los Vidrios. I was unconscious on the freeway for hours, breathing in tomato-enhancing chemical powder. Maybe that explains why I took a new job where the suffering seemed gratifying. For four years after that, I delivered I.V. bags to undocumented workers lost in the desert. I ran the routes from Agua Prieta to Douglas, from Sonoyta to Lukeville, from Nogales to Nogales (I rented a room in each of the Nogales, as if I were living in a city and its reflection). I met the *polleros* who smuggled people across the border, Immigration agents, members of the Paisano program. I never saw those who picked up the I.V. bags. The only undocumented people I ever found had already been detained. They were shivering under a blanket. They looked like Martians. Maybe the coyotes were the only ones who drank the liquid. The sum of all the corpses they find in the desert is called The Body Count. That's the title Jorge picked for the movie.

Loneliness makes you a babbler. After driving alone for ten hours, you gush words. "Being an ex-alcoholic means spinning tales," someone told me in AA. One night, after the rates went down, I called my brother. I told him a story I couldn't quite make sense of. I was driving down a dirt road when my headlights lit up two yellow silhouettes. Migrants. These ones didn't look like Martians. They looked like zombies. I braked and they put their hands up like I was going to arrest them. When they saw I was unarmed, they screamed for me to save them in the name of the Virgin and for the love of God. *They're crazy,* I thought. They were foaming at the mouth, grabbing at my shirt; they smelled like rotting cardboard. *They're already dead.* This seemed logical to me. One of them begged me to take him anywhere. The other asked for water. I didn't have a canteen. The idea of travelling with dehydrated, crazed migrants made me feel scared or disgusted or something else. But I couldn't leave them there. I told them they could ride in the back. They thought I meant the back seat. I had to use a lot more words to explain that the trunk, the boot, would be their place of travel.

I wanted to get to Phoenix by dawn. When spiny plants scratched the yellow sky, I stopped to take a leak. I didn't hear any sounds from the back. I thought the migrants had suffocated or died of thirst or hunger, but I didn't do anything. I got back in the car.

When we got to the outskirts of Phoenix, I pulled over and crossed myself. I opened the trunk, and saw the motionless bodies and the red-smeared cloth. Then I heard laughter. Only when I noticed the seeds splattered across their shirts did I remember I had been carrying three watermelons. Unbelievably, the migrants had devoured them, rinds and all. They said goodbye with a dazed happiness that left me just as troubled as the thought of accidentally murdering them.

That's the tale I told Jorge. Two days later, he called to tell me we had a "raw story." It was no good for a movie, but it was good enough to impress a producer.

My brother trusted in my knowledge of illegal crossings, and in the correspondence writing course I'd taken before becoming a trucker, when I still dreamed of being a war correspondent because it meant getting far away.

For six weeks, we sat across from each other, sweating. From his end of the table, Jorge would shout, "Producers are assholes, directors are assholes, actors are assholes!" We were writing for a commando of assholes. That was our advantage: without their knowledge, we would maneuver them into transmitting an uncomfortable truth. Jorge called it "Chaplin's whistle." In one movie, Chaplin swallows a whistle that keeps making noise inside his stomach. That's what our screenplay would be like, the whistle the assholes would swallow. There would be no way to stop it sounding off inside them.

But as if every word needed the ñ that was stuck on my keyboard, I couldn't make sense of the story. Then Jorge spoke as our father had at the table. We needed to feel guilty. We were too indifferent. We had to fuck our-selves over to deserve the story.

We went to a dogfight and bet the two thousand dollar advance. We picked a dog with an X-shaped scar on its back. It looked blind in one eye. Later we found out that rage made it wink one eye shut. We won six thousand dollars. Luck was on our side; terrible news for a screen-writer, according to Jorge.

I don't know if he took some kind of drug or pill, but I'm sure he didn't sleep. He settled back in a rocking chair on the porch, gazing at the desert acacias and the aban-doned chicken coops, the shears open across his chest. The next day, while I was stirring my instant coffee, he shouted at me with crazed eyes, "No guilt, no story!" The problem, *my* problem, was that I was already guilty. Jorge never asked me what I had been doing on that dirt road in a Spirit that didn't belong to me, and I had no desire to tell him.

When my brother had abandoned Lucía, she left with the first customer to come by the gas station. She went from one spot on the border to another, from a Jeff to a Bill to a Kevin, until there was someone called Gamaliel who seemed stable enough. He was mar-ried to another woman, but still willing to provide for Lucía. He wasn't a migrant but a "new gringo," a son of hippies who looked for baby names in the migrants' Bibles. Lucía filled me in on the details. She'd call from time to time and make sure she had my contact infor-mation, as if I were something she hoped she'd never need to make use of. A bit of insurance in the middle of nowhere.

One afternoon she called to ask me for a "big, huge favor." She needed to send a package, and I knew the roads well. Curiously, she sent me somewhere I had never been, close to Various Ranches. After that, she always used me to deliver her smaller packages. She told me they were medicine that didn't require a prescription here and was worth a lot on the other side, but she smiled in a strange way when she said it, as if "medicine" was code for money or drugs. I never opened a single envelope. That was my loyalty to Lucía. My loyalty to Jorge was not thinking too much about the breasts under her shirt, the thin, ringless hands, the eyes aching for relief.

When we'd decided to sell the farm, all six brothers got together for the first time in a long while. We fought over prices and practical details. That's when Jorge kicked the fan. He cursed us between phrases pulled from the Bible, raving about wolves and lambs, the table with a place always set for the enemy. Then he turned on the fan and heard the sound of the baby rattle. He smiled, like it was funny. This brother who'd helped me pull off my pants to feel the delicious cold of the river after a lashing now imagined himself a filmmaker esteemed enough to kick fans. I hated him like never before.

The next time Lucía called me for a delivery, I didn't leave her house till the following day. I told her my car had broken down. She loaned me the Spirit that Gamaliel had given her. I wanted to keep touching something of Lucía's, even if the car came from another man. I thought about that on the road. It made me want to leave my own mark on the Spirit. That's why I stopped to buy watermelons.

I never saw Lucía again. I returned the car when she wasn't home and I tossed the keys in the mailbox. There was an acrid taste in my mouth; I felt like breaking something. That night, I called Jorge. I told him about the zombies and the watermelons.

After six weeks, blue circles ringed my brother's eyes. He cut the dollars won at the dogfight into little squares, but that didn't bring us creative guilt either. I don't know if his concept of punishment came from life on the farm with our fanatical father, or if the drugs on the coast of Oaxaca had expanded Jorge's mind into a field for reaping regrets.

"Rob a bank," I told him.

"Crime doesn't count. We need guilt that can be overcome."

I was about to tell him I had slept with Lucía, but the chicken shears were too close.

Hours later, Jorge was smoking a twisted cigarette. It smelled like marijuana, but not enough to counter the stench of fowl. He looked at the saltpeter stain where the picture of the Virgin had been. Then he told me he was still in contact with Lucía. She had a modest business. Contraband medicine. He asked me if I had something to tell him. For the first time, I began to think the screenplay was a set-up to make me confess. Without a word, I went out to the porch and looked at the Windstar. Was it possible that the "producer" was Gamaliel, that the money and the minivan came from him? Was Jorge his messenger? Was my brother harboring someone else's jealousy? Could he have degraded himself with such precision?

I went back to my chair and wrote the whole night without stopping. I exaggerated my erotic encounters with Lucía. In this indirect confession, shamelessness could cover me. My character took on the defects of a perfect son of a bitch. To Jorge, it would have been realistic for me to act like the weak man I really was, but he couldn't credit me with such magnificent villainy. The next day, *The Body Count* was ready. It had no ñ's, but it was ready.

"You can always count on an ex-alcoholic to satisfy a vice," he told me. I didn't know if he was referring to his vice of turning guilt into film or satisfying the jealousy of others.

With the chicken shears, Jorge made some cuts to the screenplay. The most significant was my name. He made money with *The Body Count*, but it was a bland success. No one heard Chaplin's whistle.

As for me, something kept me in front of the typewriter, perhaps a line of my brother's from his last night on the farm:

"The scar is on the other ankle."

I had slept with Lucía, but I didn't remember the site of her scar. Making things up was my refuge. Was that the vice Jorge had referred to? I would keep writing. That night, I limited myself to saying,

"I'm sorry, forgive me."

I don't know if I cried. My face was wet with sweat, or tears I didn't feel. My eyes hurt. The night opened up before us, like when we were boys and we'd climb onto the roof to make wishes. A light streaked the sky.

"August 12th," Jorge said.

We spent the rest of the night watching shooting stars, like bodies lost in the desert.

MAYAN DUSK

It was the iguana's fault. We stopped in the desert next to one of those men who spend their whole lives squatting, holding three iguanas by the tail. The man we called *El Tomate,* "the Tomato," inspected the merchandise as if he knew something about green animals.

The peddler, with a face carved by sun and drought, told us that iguana blood restored sexual energy. He didn't tell us how to feed the animal because he thought we would eat it right away.

El Tomate works for a travel magazine. He lives in a ghastly building that looks out on the Viaduct. From there, he describes the beaches of Polynesia.

This time, as an exception, he really was visiting the places he would write about, Oaxaca and Yucatán. Four years earlier, we had made the trip in the opposite

direction, Yucatán–Oaxaca. Back then we were so insepa-
rable that if people saw me without him, they would ask,
"Where's El Tomate?"

We finished that last trip at the ruins of Monte Albán
during a solar eclipse. The golden stones lost their glow
and the valley was cast in a weak light that didn't belong
to any time of day. The birds sang out in bewilder-
ment and tourists took each other by the hand. I felt a
strange urge to repent, and confessed to El Tomate that
I had been the one who pushed him into the cenote at
Chichén Itzá.

That had happened a few days earlier. After seeing
the sacred water, my friend couldn't stop talking about
human sacrifices. The Mayans, superstitious about small
things, threw their midgets, their toys, their jewels, their
favorite children, all into the sacred water. I walked up
to a group of deaf-mute visitors. A woman was translating the guide's information into sign language: "He who
drinks from the cenote will return to Chichén Itzá." We
were at the water's edge, and El Tomate was leaning over
it. Something made me push him in. The rest of the trip
was an ordeal because the water gave him salmonella. At
Monte Albán, in the indeterminate light of the eclipse,
I felt bad and asked for his forgiveness. He took this as
an opportunity to ask me, "Do you really not remember
that I got you into the Silvio Rodríguez concert?" At the
beginning of our friendship, in the early seventies, El
Tomate had been the sound tech for the Mexican folk
group Aztlán. His moment of glory arrived with his
involvement in a festival of New Cuban Trova. Honestly
I didn't remember him getting me that ticket, but he told

me with a droll smile, "*I* remember." His smile irritated me because it was the same one he had when confessing he'd slept with Sonia, the Chilean refugee I'd chased around without the slightest possibility of getting into her poncho.

That reconciliation at Monte Albán was enough for us to stop seeing each other. We had crossed an invisible line.

For two years after that, we barely spoke. I didn't even call him when I found the Aztlán LP he had loaned me thirty years before. Once in a while, at the barbershop or at the dentist's office, I would find a copy of the magazine where he wrote about islands he would never see.

El Tomate got back in touch when I won the Texcoco Floral Games with a poem that I thought was pre-Raphaelite, heavily influenced by Dante Gabriel Rossetti. The prize was awarded as part of the Pulque Festival. El Tomate called at seven in the morning on the day the winner was announced. "I want to *carve a carpel from the epos,*" he exclaimed joyfully. Which meant that he wanted to go with me to the award ceremony, possibly to call in the favor of having gotten me into the questionable Silvio Rodríguez concert. I didn't respond. What he said next offended me. "López Velarde. Didn't you recognize the quote, poet?"

I said I would call him to set things up, but I never did. I imagined him in Texcoco too perfectly: gray hairs visible on the underside of his mustache, drinking a sour-smelling pulque, and declaring that my poems were terrible.

His most recent call involved the Chevy. I had filled
out a form at a Superama grocery store and won a car. I
was in the paper, an expression of primitive happiness
on my face as I accepted a set of keys that seemed to
have been fashioned for the occasion (the keychain gave
off a luxurious sparkle). El Tomate asked me to take him
from Oaxaca to Yucatán. He had to write an article. He
was sick of imagining life in five star hotels and writing
about dishes he would never taste. He wanted to plunge
into reality. "Like before," he added, inventing for us some
shared past as anthropologists or war correspondents.

Then he said, "Karla will come with us." I asked him
who she was and he became evasive. I was still recovering
from the photo of me holding the car keys appearing in
the paper and suddenly wanted to do things that might
annoy me. Also, something had happened that I needed
to get away from. A lot of time has passed but I still can't
talk about it without getting embarrassed. I'd slept with
Gloria López, who was married, and there had been an
accident unlike anything either of us had ever experi-
enced before. An improbable occurrence, like some spon-
taneous combustion that burns a body or a film negative
to ashes. My condom disappeared inside her vagina. "An
abduction," she said, more intrigued than worried. Gloria
believes in extraterrestrials. She was reasonably interested in me for the occasional roll in the hay, but she was
enormously interested in a contact of the "third kind," for
which I had been a mere intermediary.

How can indestructible rubber just disappear? She
was sure that it had something to do with aliens. Could
she get pregnant, or would the condom be encapsulated?

That verb reminded me of her favorite movie, *Fantastic Voyage,* with Raquel Welch. Gloria was too young to have seen it when it first came out. An ex-boyfriend who dedicated himself to pirating videos had awakened her to a fantasy which seemed to have been created just for her. A ship's crew is reduced to microscopic size and injected into a body to perform a complex medical operation. The body as a variant of the cosmos could only excite someone who lived to be abducted and pulled into other dimensions. "What would the internauts feel like inside of you?" Gloria asked with the seriousness of someone who considers such a thing to be possible. "Is there anything kinkier than having internauts in your veins?" The movie's producers were thinking the same thing when they chose Rachel Welch and dressed her in an extremely tight white suit. The sexual nonsense of a tiny turgid body advancing through your blood seduced Gloria, who now felt crewed by the condom that had ended up inside her. It didn't help to recall that the original seamen exited the body through a tear duct, a metaphor announcing that all adventures of intravenous seduction end in tears. On top of all this was the possibility that Gloria's husband would find this improbable intruder by *the way of all flesh* (Alluding to Samuel Butler doesn't diminish the grotesqueness of the topic, I know, but at least it's too highbrow for El Tomate's taste).

Though there is no greater relief than knowing someone else has encountered the same predicament and developed home remedies, I was too ashamed to talk about it. I was experiencing the anxiety of having to face a pregnancy or an enraged husband, plus the fact that my accomplice was distracted by extraterrestrial intrigue, when El Tomate suggested we take a trip. I accepted on the spot.

Karla decided to ride in the back seat because she had read *The System of Objects* by Baudrillard and that part of the car made her feel "deliciously dependent." In every other way she was a pro-independence fury. She wouldn't accept our schedules, nor did she believe that the highway had the number of miles indicated on the map.

Luckily she was asleep for a good part of the trip. In one of the backwater towns, we bought the iguana.

When Karla woke up, near Pinotepa Nacional, she saw the iguana, and we dropped a few notches in her esteem. There are King Kong men, obsessed with blondes, and then there are Godzilla men, obsessed with monsters. The former complex is racial, the latter phallic. We had bought a dinosaur to our own scale. For fifty miles, she tried to explain what was authentic and what wasn't.

Karla had a strange way of scratching her belly, very slowly, as if she wasn't soothing her stomach but her hand. She lifted up her shirt enough to reveal a tattoo like a second navel in the shape of a yin-yang.

Once we got to Oaxaca, the iguana stuck out its tongue, round as a peanut. Karla suggested we give it something to eat and El Tomate got to use the inscrutable saying: "Now we'll know which side the iguana chews on." We had all heard it before, without ever trying to under-stand it.

We bought dried flies in a tropical fish store, then left the iguana in the car with a ration of insects that it either ate or lost on the floor.

It was two in the afternoon, and El Tomate picked a restaurant he had written epic poems about without ever having been there. It was hard to get Karla to accept a table. All of them violated some aspect of *feng shui*. We ate on the patio, next to a well that would give us energy. Karla practiced "mystical decor." That's what her business card said, from when she had lived in Cancún. She had just moved to Mexico City and El Tomate had put her up. She was the daughter of an acquaintance who had gotten pregnant at 16. From the moment my friend greeted me, making a gun with his forefinger and thumb, I knew the trip was an excuse to get into Karla's pants.

El Tomate's morality runs in zig-zags. He would have considered it an abuse to sleep with his guest in Mexico City, but not in Oaxaca and Yucatán.

I didn't want to eat yellow mole and El Tomate accused me of hating authenticity. It's possible that I hate authenticity; either way, I hate yellow food. When he went to the bathroom, Karla turned her hyperobjective interest to me. "And how are you doing now?" she asked. I supposed that El Tomate had told her about a tremendous "before." She paused and added, in a complicit tone, "I get the iguana thing."

Emotions are confusing. I liked that she looked at me as if I were a piece of moveable furniture. I acknowledged that I had had some rough times, but said I was now doing better. I talked to the crumbs on her plate. Then I looked up at her chestnut eyes. She ruined her smile by saying, "He worries about you a lot." Of course she meant El Tomate. It bothered me that he could become a pronoun and take advantage of my deterioration to play the caring friend. What had he told Karla? That I voluntarily committed myself to the San Rafael Psychiatric Institute while he danced revolutionary Chilean *cuecas* with Sonia? That much was true. Plus, in the search for pre-Raphaelite exaltation, I had started on a fast that led me to semi-dementia. But El Tomate had invented other eccentricities. Karla spoke to me like the Yaquí Indian Don Juan to Carlos Castaneda: "Everyone has his inner animal." She touched my hand with compassion.

There was a classical music festival going on in Oaxaca City and we could only find one room for the three of us, in a bed and breakfast on the outskirts of town, near the Tule Tree. We saw the centuries-old trunk in whose knots Italo Calvino had discovered an intricate alphabet, and in which a guide found other representations. "There is Olga Breeskin's backside," he said and pointed to something that looked like the exaggerated posterior of a *vedette*.

The iguana passed through various stages. In its Oaxaca phase, its only thought was to flee from us. There were two beds in the room: a double that Karla assigned to us, and hers. The armoire was a solid monstrosity from the era of the Mexican Revolution. No amount of *feng shui* could move it. That's where the iguana slept, or more accurately, that's where we wanted it to sleep. In the middle of the night, I heard the scratching of claws. I went to the armoire and saw that the iguana had disappeared. Something told me it wasn't in the room. The door had a rope-tie instead of a lock. I know there's no logic to my reasoning, but a door tied closed with a rope suggests a multitude of problems. I went out into the hall, which led to the only bathroom in the hotel. I found the iguana in the toilet. Had it gone there to drink water? According to El Tomate, iguanas hydrate with certain fruits we had not found but which did apparently exist. The iguana slipped between my legs. I chased it with the intensity of an insomniac, forgetting I hadn't the slightest interest in capturing it. I found it in the foyer, next to a copy of a sculpture from Mitla, an old man in a funerary pose. Maybe that squatting priest reminded it of its old owner; the fact is, it stayed still and I was able to trap it. It bit me hard enough to draw blood. I squeezed its snout closed like I was wringing out a towel and returned to the room with my prey. El Tomate had taken the opportunity to jump into Karla's bed, but when I opened the door everything was just as quiet and as un-*feng shui* as before I had left.

In the morning, the bite appeared on my hand in a charismatic manner. It looked like I had pricked myself with thorns made of light. Karla got wonderfully concerned and put Tiger Pomade on me.

I called Gloria that morning to see if there was any news of the "fantastic voyager." "Not yet," she answered sourly. She was furious because she had lost her passport. She blamed me for never committing to anything. She didn't have the slightest interest in my commitment to the condom lost in her interior—what she wanted was for me to commit to finding her passport.

On our last trip, we were warned. "They're going to mug you in the Isthmus of Tehuantepec." That time we were traveling by bus, The Turquoise Arrow or Star of the Morning line. They mugged us right there on the bus. One man threatened the driver with a machete while the other went through our pockets. I remember his blood-shot eyes and the mezcal on his breath when he said, "It's your lucky day. Just imagine, you could've gone off a cliff."

This time around, they mugged us without our real-izing it. We were pumping gas in the mountains. It was nighttime; Karla and the iguana were sleeping in the back of the car. El Tomate was staring out into infinity from the front seat.

The gas station attendant asked me if I was going to Yucatán and began to tell me a legend. The Jaguar has spots on his body because he bit into the sun. When he had finished up all the light in Oaxaca, he went on to Yucatán, but he couldn't keep eating fire because a Mayan prince fought him and the two of them drowned together in the sacred cenote. Their bodies floated through the underground rivers of the peninsula until they reached the sea. That's why the Caribbean has those strange phosphorescent lights. We Mexicans don't know that the phosphorescence is valuable, but the Japanese come in boats to steal it. The story lasted long enough for the attendant's accomplices to make off with my rear lights. El Tomate didn't notice anything because he was "thinking about time."

We took the highway out of the mountains, heading east. Every so often a semi passed me, honking alarm-ingly. I only connected this to the lack of rear lights when we got to the hotel in Villahermosa and I went to check the car. "What kind of idiot are you?" I asked El Tomate. I didn't notice the theft either, but at least I had been busy listening to the Mayan legend. Why would the Japanese want marine phosphorescence? Is it nutritious? I thought about how easy it is to trick someone like me. Strangely, I thought better of El Tomate. He looked at me with disarming sadness. "Can I tell you something?" he asked.

He didn't wait for my answer to tell me that before we left Mexico City, he had burned off the warts on his chest. "I felt so old with those warts." He lifted up his shirt to show me his burns, like some Xipe Totec, the Aztec Flayed God. Obviously he had scorched himself for the benefit of Karla.

The other news was that the iguana had vanished in the Ithsmus. We took the suitcases and Karla's water bottles out of the car, but there was no sign of it.

In Villahermosa, we stayed in a couple of bungalows with terraces. Every so often, a waiter would come by to offer us a drink. Karla went to bed early because she was exhausted from sleeping through the highway's winding curves.

El Tomate and I smoked a couple of dry cigars we had bought from a man selling paper flowers. We drank rum until very late. We had reached that friendly lethargy in which it's acceptable to not say anything at all. We could hear crickets, night birds, and, very far off, the satisfying sound of insects frying themselves on an electric lantern. El Tomate broke the peace: "Why don't you go get her?"

I thought he was talking about the iguana, but his eyes were fixed on Karla's bungalow. He scratched his bare chest. I stared at the ruddy stains. "They put liquid nitrogen on me," he explained, like a futuristic martyr. He had burned himself to impress Karla, his warts had smoldered in a sacrificial rite, but now he was asking me to go after her. "It's obvious she likes you. She hasn't moved a single chair in two days," his words came out bitterly, like the last mouthful of bad tobacco.

It had always been depressing to imagine my friend in his apartment next to the traffic off the Viaduct, writing about Roman churches and Sicilian ruins. Now there was nothing sadder than seeing him on this trip, devastatingly real.

"We already know which side the iguana chews on," he added with a resigned smile.

When I got back to the room, something shifted inside me. The poverty of the scene—the tiny Rosa Venus soap, the rusty bottle opener, the ashtray bearing the name of some other hotel—made me realize that I was also in a bad state. It upset me that El Tomate would encourage me to approach Karla. I remembered the time he was carrying around the sound equipment for the band Aztlán. He took advantage of his privileged access to that music (flutes played in outrage over squalor) to sleep with Sonia. Now he was offering me a different woman to make up for his disloyalty. Or maybe he was playing another hand, maybe he needed to take advantage of the trip, to secure the possibility of complaining about me in the future. If I slept with Karla, his subsequent blackmail could be implacable, a rarefied cruelty, like the mood of a Mayan god.

He was right about one thing: Karla had stopped moving the furniture around, and not just that: at every restaurant she opened the packets of saltines, spread butter on them, and passed them to me without asking.

I washed myself in the dribble of water that fell from the showerhead. It was the prelude to a disastrous journey. We visited the ruins of Palenque. The guide wanted us to see the carving of an "astronaut" in the inner chamber of a pyramid. The "controls" of the "ship" were ears of corn.

"Nothing is authentic," muttered El Tomate. The whole day, he kept looking at me as if I had just emerged from the bungalow he had told me to enter.

Karla noticed something was wrong between us and distracted herself by humming an indecipherable melody. We rushed through the brick ruins of Comalcalco, ate alligator-headed fish without acknowledging the strange flavor, and made our way towards the mesa of Mayan kings.

We were passing through a region of dry shrubs crowned with purple flowers when a strange rattling came from the front hood of the car. I thought it was the belt, or one of the many parts of the motor I didn't understand.

When I raised the hood in front of us, Karla embraced me, kissed me. And there was the iguana, looking at us with prehistoric patience, its tail beating against the spark plugs like a metronome. The animal was hot, but I trapped it with the anxiousness that Karla had stirred up.

In Maní, I checked out the car while they drank *horchatas*. The iguana had made a hole in the back of the rear seat. From there, it got into the chassis and made its way to the motor. The animal represented my karma, my aura, my very being. It was also gnawing holes in my car.

We visited the Temple of San Miguel de Maní, where Fray Diego de Landa ordered the Mayan codices to be burned. The cosmogony of a people had gone up in sententious flames. I told Karla about the things that are lost and the things that remain. The iguana belonged in this setting, like the burned codices. It had to reintegrate itself into this reality. I didn't need it anymore. Karla gave me a highly charged look, the kind you give someone who has been hospitalized because of guilt or complicity with his inner animals. In front of Karla, El Tomate had turned me into an interesting case of fantastical zoology. I looked up at the Yucatecan sky, pure blue, and felt I was able to talk about creative loss. After burning the codices, Fray Diego wrote the history of the Mayans. I would make a similar restitution. The liberation of the iguana would allow me to break through my writer's block. I had a cycle of poems in mind, "The Green Circle," an allusion to the iguana biting its own tail and the Mayans inventing the zero. "You only possess the things you lose voluntarily," I thought, but I didn't say it out loud because it was pedantic and because El Tomate was watching me from a distance, making a gun with his forefinger and thumb. This time, the gesture meant he approved of my proximity to Karla.

We arrived at the Yucatán phase of the iguana. If in Oaxaca it had wanted to flee, now it wanted to be with us. We unsuccessfully freed it in front of the Church of the Three Kings of Tizimín; among the pale stones of the immense atrium of Izamal; under the laurel trees in the Mérida's main square. It wasn't drawn to the greenery that surrounded the cenote at Dzibilchaltún either. It kept coming back to us, domesticated by our delicious flies, by the Chevy and its innumerable holes. "Animals hate authenticity," I told El Tomate.

That afternoon I called Gloria. "It finally came out," she told me. I felt a cosmic relief. She, however, was not in a good mood. "Now I want to know which part of me my passport is going to come out of." I knew that the only thing that tied us together were the problems I could cause her.

When I hung up, I saw Karla in the distance, standing on a rock. Her silhouette had a strange immobility. Her body, agile and tense, didn't seem to be at rest; she was gathering energy to jump.

Near the archeological site of Chichén Itzá, we found a little hotel that was part of a Brahman cattle ranch. We had been driving the whole afternoon, facing into the sun. El Tomate had a tremendous migraine. He went to bed early and Karla said to me, "I thought of a name for the iguana."

I put my finger on her lips so she wouldn't say "Odysseus" or "Xóchitl" or "Tao." She kissed me softly. That night I caressed her yin-yang tattoo until morning.

I went back to my room when dawn broke. I saw fragile trees with intricate fronds. A blue bird was singing in the branches. The white cattle were grazing on the flat land. I felt happy and guilty. By the time I got back to my room, I just felt guilty. I had pushed El Tomate into the water because I could never stand that Sonia preferred him to me; he'd had the decency to forgive me, and I had paid him back in false coin. To top it off, I had remembered that it was him who got me into that Silvio Rodríguez concert. El Tomate felt old. It had been years since he'd had a stable relationship, he had burned off his warts like a punitive Aztec. I thought about different ways to approach him. They were all unnecessary: he had slipped a note under the door. "I understand. I would have done the same thing. We'll see each other in Mexico City." That note situated him mysteriously beside us, as if he had been spying on us the whole night.

I visited Chichén Itzá in a zombie state. Karla told me she knew I was in love with her when she caught me staring strangely while we ate *buñuelos* outside the Santo Domingo Convent in Oaxaca. The truth is, I was looking at her strangely because the iguana was insisting on biting me in the same place it had already bitten me.

We climbed the 91 stairs of the Pyramid of Kukulcán; neither the heat nor the exertion impeded conversation. She told me she had left Cancún because she was sick of her suitors. Then she pointed at a gringo in a Hawaiian shirt who hadn't stopped taking pictures of her. She felt harassed by the unfulfilled desires of others. Only El Tomate, who was old and a consummate gentleman, had treated her with egalitarian friendship.

When we got to the cenote, I felt even worse. El Tomate had drunk the water, but the prophecy of returning was being fulfilled by me. Perhaps wrongful immersion brings about such consequences.

In that moment, I hated archeological guides. They were like deep sea fish. They had swollen eyelids and talked about things they didn't understand. There were so many, it was impossible not to hear what came out of their heads, so full of murky water. At the Tzompantli, the Place of Skulls, one of the guides said that the Mayans brought iguanas on their journeys. They skinned them alive because meat rots quickly in the heat of Yucatán. On the steps of the *sacbé*, the white road that joins the sacred cities, they would tear off chunks of meat and continue traveling. As long as the iguana's heart kept beating, they could eat bits of its body. Then they ate the heart. The guide smiled with his fishy teeth.

I felt a hole in my stomach. Karla painstakingly bit her nails. I bought green mangos but she didn't want to try them. We saw the delicate skulls of the Tzompantli, the stone writing of those legible buildings in a language that had been lost. I thought about the bleeding iguana that fed the Mayan pilgrims. A sensation of loss, of diffuse horror came over me. The iguana followed us, our unlikely pet. I remembered how much I owed El Tomate. In his way, he wanted to do me a favor by disappearing at dawn like the Lone Ranger. Karla looked at the sky to avoid seeing the iguana. "The guides lie," I told her. "They're blind fish." She didn't ask me to explain. She must have been thinking something terrible; her body shook, stuck in a shudder. Maybe it wasn't the Mayan cruelty that shocked her so much as the effect of the story, the way in which it intersected our journey. El Tomate had sold me to her as an attractive problem he couldn't fully fathom, or one which had already exceeded him.

She lifted my hand off her shoulder. "I have to think," she said, as if ideas came to her through touch.

By the time we got to the cenote, it was getting dark. The iguana changed course when it saw four or five members of its own species on the wet earth surrounding the pool. There, it left us.

The Chevy was waiting in the parking lot. I thought about the things that are destroyed so that poetry can exist. I thought about Yeats and the impossible, sacrificial love of Celts. I thought about my inability to sink deep like the dusk.

Karla wanted to sit in the back seat. I asked her to sit next to me. This time she did not cite *The System of Objects.* "It's the seat of death," she said. "I'm not your chauffeur," I answered sharply. Scared, she obeyed.

We crashed three curves outside of Chichén Itzá. The brakes didn't respond. The cables had been gnawed straight through. Karla broke two ribs, puncturing her lung. The Chevy was totaled. I was unhurt except for the bite I already had on my hand.

Sometimes I think Karla stopped talking to me because I was unharmed, and that gave intentionality to the accident. Too many times she said, "It wasn't your fault." Everything had been wrong from before we'd entered the car, or from a moment before that, already irrecoverable. What design were we fulfilling when we shared our breath and believed we could search for ourselves in two bodies?

I tried in vain to write "The Green Circle." Over long afternoons, the only thing I did was sketch an animal.

El Tomate published his report with stupendous photos of Oaxaca and Yucatán. When I read it, I remembered the nape of Karla's neck, the skin on her back glowing in that light that only exists on the peninsula.

That night, I saw her in my dreams. I asked her what the iguana's name was, but I didn't dream her answer.

ORDER SUSPENDED

For Manuel Felguérez

Rosalía has more than enough to worry about. She lights a candle for the Russians trapped in their submarine (they were communicating by banging a metal door with their tools, they didn't have much oxygen left, and the sea was freezing). She's like that. She prays for Russians she doesn't know, who won't be saved.

I hate spots. I huffed too much glue in high school and one night I understood that the spots on my arms were spiders embedded in my skin. I tried to cut them out with a knife. My father kicked me in the face and saved me. He also broke my jaw. They wired it shut and I spent weeks drinking soup through a straw. Quitting glue isn't easy. You wake up and your fingernails are full of plaster dust from scratching the walls all night. "Only pain makes you feel better," my father told me.

It's true. His kick put me on a new path. I didn't go back to school, where the teacher had told us, "Study, boys, or you'll end up being journalists." I wanted to sink down into journalism. Instead, I rose up on a scaffold as a window cleaner.

In front of the building, Jacinto sours life with his lottery tickets. He fell off a scaffold centuries ago. Now he's a gimp promising good fortune. I've seen blind men, crippled men, hunchbacked men selling lottery tickets— like they were fucked over so you could win. None of them ever buys a ticket.

The building is *intelligent*. The lights go on when you walk down a hallway; in the elevator, a voice says the names of the floors and the companies that occupy them. The voice is sexy and cold. A soldier woman. "The building sees more signs than you do," Rosalía complains. She thinks I'm insensitive: "You're fuckin' deprived." I'm too deprived to see the things that interest her, but I did notice that the elevator voice talks just like a warrior woman I saw on TV. The Japanese listened to her, closed their eyes, and took delight in dying.

"You don't see signs," she insists.

"Signs of what?" I ask.

"Signs of anything."

Rosalía smells like something ocean-y, foamy. The sheet rises over her nose when she sleeps. I've been collecting 20 peso bills for years. I stick them in a plastic Spiderman doll I won in a raffle. It came full of powdered hot chocolate. The doll reminds Rosalía that one afternoon I had good aim. I think about the blue bills inside it, a tight sea, held in place.

*   *   *

I don't like the city from the scaffold but I like that it's behind me. A vibrating mass. Every scaffold has two operators. I go up and down with a guy we call El Chivo, the Goat. El Chivo smokes all day. He smokes because inside the building there's no smoking and because the cigarettes are called Wings.

El Chivo is a veteran. The first day he explained what he calls "the method:" You shouldn't look down or to the side; what you should watch is your own face in the glass. That's what you're cleaning, your reflection.

It's almost impossible to see through the glass because of the reflective coating. Sometimes I look and look and I see something inside. That's how I spotted the painter in the meeting room on Floor 18. He was standing in front of a huge white canvas. I saw him put the first spot on it. I hate spots, as I said before, but I couldn't stop staring at the black paint beginning to drip. I felt strange, like those spots were the sins I carried inside me. I wanted to clean them like I wanted to get the spiders out from under my skin. Then the painter started to use other colors. All earth tones, but very different. How many colors make up the Earth? I calmed myself by staring at a spot that was rusted. Like mud made from rotted metal toys. I looked so hard I thought a blood spot might appear in the white of my eye, like the one Rosalía has. It's a mole. Sometimes she says it appeared on its own, other times she says a piece of charcoal fell into her eye when she was a girl. I think she saw something she's not telling me about. That's why she looks at things like they're signs.

"It's abstract," El Chivo said, as if he could see better from his part of the scaffold. "Do you know what abstract is?"

I didn't answer him. I know I don't see signs. That's what abstract is.

"Don't you think it's nuts that spots get a name? One spot isn't called anything, but a bunch of spots get a title." He pointed to the painting through the glass.

El Chivo never stops talking, like his tongue is full of spines he can't quite spit out.

"Together the spots mean more than just spots."

"Spot on!" I said.

He kept talking. He needs so many words to tell a story that's always the same: when he was a boy his father used to lock him down in a storm drain.

"Do you know what the sky looks like from a storm drain?" he asks me and I always tell him I don't. "It's three lines. A grate." Then he smiles, and even though he's missing teeth, he looks happy up there on the scaffold. The storm drain made him happy to be outside. That's his real method. The fucked up part of the story is that now he works to support his "Pops" who trapped him in the storm drain. El Chivo doesn't have a wife or kids. Not even a dog to wag its tail at him. He lives for his Pops who gulps down money and medicine. El Chivo is always asking to borrow cash. He comes to me with his tongue hanging out, like he can smell the money I keep in the Spiderman. A goddamn dog for money. You can treat him bad and say no a thousand times and he still hangs out his tongue.

Sometimes I dream about karate-fight fog. The men are fighting in a cold part of Japan. I'm their guru. They kneel before me. I give each of them a different cleaning product to smell. That's how I decide who beats the shit out of whom, and how.

I woke up and saw a mold spot on the ceiling. It was shaped like Alaska. Why do mold spots have shapes? If not Alaska, they look like Australia. I had a thought that the painter was painting against those types of spots. He wanted to make spot-spots that couldn't be anything else. Not spider-spots or geography-spots.

The next day the wind blew so hard it made the scaffold creak. I've never seen a bird fly as high up as we are. They float down below. They look like black garbage pushed by the wind.

Outside the 18th floor, I leaned in to see the painting. The painter moved his spots around and then, when he backed up to view them, they moved a little more, like they weren't fixed, or like they were going to burst. One part was as brown and powdery as the chocolate I removed from the Spiderman. I closed my eyes and saw the sea. Rosalía was sinking slowly, wrapped in a plant with Jell-O-like leaves.

I descended half asleep. The Chief Intendant was waiting for us. The news he had was splitting his face with happiness. He took us into the lobby. People eyed our harnesses with great respect. There was a feeling like something was about to happen. On one screen, a video was being projected. A gringo named Melvin was going to climb our building. He was training to climb the Kuala Lumpur Towers. Our building was the height of the "knee" of Kuala Lumpur. He would have to climb ours several times to be prepared. They asked him why he didn't climb mountains and he said, "Buildings are more virgin." Then we saw the sharp, golden towers, like sky-high pagodas that fed on light: "Kuala Lumpur."

The Chief Intendant informed us that we would spend a week inside the building, clearing the terrain for the climber. They sent me to clean the meeting room; El Chivo was assigned the first floor.

The Chief knows Rosalía. I got the job because he's the *compadre* of someone in the neighborhood who admires Rosalía. The Chief doesn't admire me. "With any luck, he'll fall." That's how he told her he was giving me the job.

They announced there would be a party for the employees. TV crews were coming to promote our building. Rosalía was going to participate, too. She works in a bakery and our night watchman recommended it. We were going to cut one cake shaped like the Kuala Lumpur Towers and another shaped like our building.

Rosalía had counted the days the Russians were in the submarine, until they asphyxiated at the bottom of the sea. She worries about far away things. You ask her how she's doing and you never know if she's answering for herself.

That week, Rosalía could only think about the climber, about how he might die for something meaningless. They are no Olympics for building climbing. Melvin was risking his life just because. Afterwards, everyone would forget about him like they had with the Russians in the submarine.

*   *   *

Rosalía made an enormous cake. We were going to eat cake simply because someone had dared to dangle above us. I liked seeing her so worked up, thinking about her cake and the moments when strangers sink with no hope, or climb very high with no explanation. Then I thought about our trip to the sea. A surprise isn't exactly a sign, but at least I would give her something unexpected.

What I liked most about working inside the building was looking at the tower across the street. Made out of glass. Almost invisible. Only the orange sparkle of the sun revealed where the glass stopped and the air began.

I wanted to light a cigarette but didn't dare. The painter, they let smoke. He puffed on cigar tobacco that he put in a pipe. He likes to turn one thing into another. His spots had turned into blocks. They looked like a map. A map without geography.

The painter got used to me walking around cleaning things that were already clean. He told me something was souring with the painting. He wanted to disorganize it, but it kept rearranging itself, like it was being pulled from the inside. *Magnets,* I thought. The colors came together as if drawn by inner forces. I saw a red dot in a bucket of paint and thought about Rosalía's mole. What would she see in the painting? She had so much imagination, she was sure to find more than I could. I felt something like vertigo and remembered El Chivo's "method." Don't look to the side or down, just straight ahead: your reflection. Deep in the world of the painting, everything vibrated, as if it could recede forever but the colors would remain because they were fighting against it, whatever it was that was falling.

Signs. It was exciting to sense something that I couldn't articulate to Rosalía. Then I looked at the glass walls and I saw the climber. The walls were starting to fog up on the outside. He looked blurry. He had suction pads to hold onto the glass.

The day of the party, we ate Rosalía's cakes. Our building wore a sombrero and the Kuala Lumpur towers had strange little hats she'd copied out of a magazine. They talked about us on TV. El Chivo and I went up to the roof and lowered down a slice of cake on a rope to Melvin the climber.

Rosalía stayed on after the party. El Chivo, who was mopping the first floor, told her the same story three times.

That night Rosalía was affectionate with me in a sad way, like I had just returned from spear-fishing sharks but she really loved me and didn't care that I smelled bad and was missing an arm.

"Why didn't you give it to him?" she asked while I was falling asleep.

In the early morning I heard crying, or maybe it was one of the karate fighters moaning in my dreams.

Two days later, El Chivo won the lottery. Jacinto had sold him the winning ticket. Tears ran down his face as he told us he was putting his Pops in a private clinic. There are faces that are ruined when things go well. El Chivo's was like that. I couldn't look at him anymore and went out to the street.

Jacinto came up to me as soon as he saw me. He started talking about El Chivo.

"I told him those were lucky bills. They smelled like chocolate."

So Rosalía knew my secret, the bills that I was saving. She didn't want to find out what I might use them for. She'd given them to El Chivo like he was one of the Russians in the submarine.

That night, when I got home, I pointed to the Spiderman. Rosalía came right up to me and bared her neck, showing me a very fine vein, as if she were a small animal that I could kill with a single bite.

"His pain won me over," she said later.

I had gone up and down on the scaffold hearing the same question every day. "Do you know what the sky looks like from a storm drain?" Hearing it once was enough for her.

She didn't ask me why I'd been hiding the money. I could have told her it was to go to the sea, but I kept quiet. Maybe she would have preferred to give it to El Chivo anyway.

I spent the night listening to the sound of airplanes in the sky. I wondered what would happen if I soaked Rosalía with a can of gasoline or if I threw El Chivo off the scaffold. When the sun came up, I was carefully stroking an ice pick.

The first floor was full of flowers and candles.

"He fell," Jacinto said to me.

I didn't understand.

"The goddamn gringo."

Three women were crying in the corner where Rosalía's cake had been.

I saw a spot on the sidewalk, a stretched spot, a spot with lots of arms and legs, as if the blood had been in a hurry to spill out and fill several bodies.

I went up to Floor 18. The painter had finished the painting.

"Can I smell it?" I asked him.

He let me get my nose up close. It smelled like the world, the world from the inside. I asked him if it had a name.

"Order Suspended," he said.

The building has eight parking lots underground and pilings that sink further down and protect it from earthquakes. Everything floats up from there: *"Order Suspended."*

I looked at the painting and it was like the colors had reorganized themselves. I saw plaster dust under fingernails, three bars of light, the grate, the sky from a storm drain, the golden spires of Kuala Lumpur, the blood mole, the grainy chocolate powder, the sheet over Rosalía's face, rising and falling with her breath, the black charcoal that had hurt her, the clean circle of a suction cup on glass, the blood stretched out on the sidewalk. I saw the fog in my dream, I saw the earth under the earth, the magnet that pulled everything together like the curve of fate. I wanted something badly without knowing what it was. Someone could paint all of that. I could clean the spots.

Rosalía had lit candles for the Russian marines. She could love what she had never seen. She could help a mouth with no teeth. El Chivo's mouth. The climber's death was going to be worse for her than for me. I didn't understand what she carried inside that made her like that, but I needed her because of it. I felt the ice pick in the pocket of my overalls.

"I was going to kill somebody, but somebody else died," I told the painter.

That was only half true. I liked the idea of killing El Chivo, but I was going to go up and down with him my whole life without killing him, stroking the ice pick, just like I went up and down before without lending him money.

The painter looked at me as if he didn't believe me, or he understood everything, or I was a painting.

The building's windows were dirty. Here and there, you could see clean circles: the climber's suction cups.

I hung with El Chivo on the scaffold. He said they had hooked his father up to a tube. He described a kind of vacuum capable of blowing into a man, like that was happiness. *It's his fault, his damn fault,* I thought, but what I said was:

"That's good."

He didn't hear me, or he didn't know what I meant.

"Okey dokey!" I shouted to him up there on the scaffold, several times because there was a lot of wind. He seemed to understand that I was resigned or that I believed in luck. I felt like I was pulling a spot out from under my skin.

That day he didn't tell the story about his father. When we finished cleaning, he hugged me.

"Thank you," he said. The words whistled through his missing teeth. He smelled like Windex and sweat, like we all smell. Then he handed me three blue bills: "Your change." He smiled.

Jacinto came up to us on the street. He offered me a lottery ticket. I remembered the title of the painting, *Order Suspended.* Jacinto had been fucked over to sell fortune, I had lost so someone else could win, and Rosalía had given money without losing anything. "Signs," I said to myself, and then, for the first time, I played the lotto.

AMIGOS MEXICANOS

1. *Katzenberg*

The phone rang twenty times. The caller must have been thinking that I live in a villa where it takes forever to get from the stables to the phone, or that there's no such thing as cordless phones here, or that I experience fits of mystic uncertainty and have a hard time deciding to pick up the receiver. That last one was true, I'm sorry to say.

It was Samuel Katzenberg. He had come back to Mexico to do a story on violence. Last visit, he'd been traveling on *The New Yorker*'s dime. Now he was working for *Point Blank,* one of those publications that perfume their ads and print how-to's on being a man of the world. It took him two minutes to tell me the move was an improvement.

"In Spanish, point blank is '*a quemarropa.*'" Katzenberg hadn't grown tired of showing off how well he spoke the language. "The magazine doesn't just publish fluff pieces; my editor looks for serious stories. She's a very cool *mujer*, a one-woman *fiesta*. Mexico is magical, but confusing. I need your help to figure out which parts are horrible and which parts are Buñuel-esque." He tongued the ñ as if he were sucking on a silver bullet and offered me a thousand dollars.

Then I explained why I was offended.

Two years earlier, Samuel Katzenberg had come to do his bazillionth story on Frida Kahlo. Someone told him I wrote scripts for "hard-hitting" documentaries, and he'd paid me to escort him through a city he deemed savage and explain things he deemed mythical.

Katzenberg had read extensively on the heartwrenching work of Mexican painters. He knew more than I did about murals with twenty-foot-long ears of corn, the Museo de la Revolución, the assassination attempt on Trotsky, the fleeting romance between Frida and the Soviet prophet during his exile in Coyoacán. Pedantically, he explained to me the importance of the "wound as a transsexual construct:" the paralyzed painter was sexy in a way that was "very postmodern, beyond gender." Logically, Madonna admired her without understanding her.

In preparation for that first trip, Katzenberg had interviewed professors of cultural studies at Brown, Princeton, and Duke. He had done his homework. The next step consisted of establishing definitive contact with Frida's *true* country. He hired me to be his contact with the genuine. But it was hard for me to satisfy his appetite for authenticity. In his mind, everything I showed him was either a gaudy farce for tourists, or something ghastly with no local color. He wanted a reality that was like Frida's paintings, ghastly but unique. Katzenberg didn't understand that her famous traditional dresses were now only to be found on the second floor of the Museo de Antropología, or worn on godforsaken ranches where they were never as luxurious or finely embroidered. He also didn't understand that today's Mexican woman takes pains to wax the honest mustache that, according to him, made F.K. (Katzenberg loved abbreviations) a bisexual icon.

It didn't help that nature decided to thrust an environmental disaster into his story. The volcano Popocatépetl had become active again, and we visited Frida's mansion under a rain of ash. This let me muse with calculated nostalgia on the disappearance of the sky, so central to life in Mexico City.

"We've lost the most transparent region of the air," I commented, as if pollution also meant the end of Aztec lyricism.

I'll admit I stuffed Katzenberg full of clichés and vernacular flashiness. But it was his fault. He wanted to see iguanas in the streets.

Mexico disappointed him, as if the whole country were some ceremonial site, commercialized and in ruins, full of peddlers hawking tanning oil to sun worshippers.

I introduced him to an expert on Mexican art and Katzenberg refused to talk with him. I should have quit right then; I couldn't tolerate working for a racist. Didier Morand was black, from Senegal. He had come to Mexico when then-President Luis Echeverría decided that our countries were deeply alike. Didier wore beaded necklaces and beautiful African tunics. He was a Commissary of Mexican Art, and very few people knew as much as he did. But Katzenberg was annoyed that he'd honor so many cultures at once.

"I don't need an African source." He looked at me as if I were trying to sell him the wrong ethnicity.

I decided to cut him down to size: I asked for double the money.

He accepted, and so I tried my best to find metaphors and adjectives that would bring out the essential Mexico, or something that could represent it in his eyes, so hungry for "genuine" disasters.

That's when I introduced him to Gonzalo Erdiozábal.

Gonzalo looks like a fiery Moor from 1940s Hollywood. He radiates the hyperdignified elegance of a Sultan who's lost his camels and has no plans to get them back. Or at least, that's how we see him in Mexico. In Europe, he seems very Mexican. For four years in the 80s, he managed to get himself worshipped in Austria as Xochipili, a supposed descendent of the Emperor Moctezuma. Every morning, he'd go to the Ethnographic Museum of Vienna dressed as an Aztec dancer, light copal incense, and ask for signatures supporting the repossession of Moctezuma's headdress, whose quetzal feathers were languishing there in a glass case.

In his role as Xochipili, Gonzalo showed the Austrian populace that what they thought of as a charmless gift from Emperor Maximilian was actually a piece of our identity. He gathered enough signatures to bring the issue to Parliament, raising funds from NGOs and winning the boundless devotion of a shifting harem of blondes. Obviously, it would have been a disaster if he'd actually repossessed the headdress. His cause only prospered so long as the Austrians postponed handing it over. He was able to enjoy his "Moctezuma fellowship" without being defeated by the generosity of his adversaries: it was nostalgia that forced him to come back before he could claim the imperial plumes ("I miss the reek of pork rinds and gasoline," he wrote me.)

When Katzenberg doubled my salary, I called Gonzalo and offered him one third. Gonzalo cobbled together a fertility rite on a concrete rooftop, and took us to the shack of a splotchy-skinned clairvoyant who made us gnaw on sugarcane so she could read our destinies in the pulp.

Thanks to Gonzalo's improvised traditions, Katzenberg found the local color he needed for his story. On our last night together, he had one too many tequilas and confessed that the magazine had given him an expense account fat enough to live for a month, like a king. Gonzalo and I had made it possible for him to "research" everything in just one week.

The next day, he was back to scrimping. He decided the hotel shuttle was too expensive so he flagged down a parrot-green VW. The taxi driver took him down an alley and held a screwdriver to his jugular. Katzenberg was left with nothing but his passport and his plane ticket, but his flight was canceled because Popocatépetl started erupting and ashes had clogged the planes' turbines.

He spent one last day in Mexico City, watching news reports on the volcano, too scared to even go out into the hallway. He called and asked me to come see him. I was afraid he was going to ask me to give him back the money, and even more afraid I'd offer it to him. I told him I was busy because a witch had put the evil eye on me.

I felt bad for Katzenberg, long distance, until he sent me a copy of the story he'd written. The title's vulgar pun wasn't the worst of it: "There She Blows: Frida and the Volcano." I was in the piece, described as "one of the locals." Somehow, though he hadn't deigned to dignify me with a name, Katzenberg had included every word I'd said, unhampered by quotation marks or scruples. His story was a pillage of my ideas. His only originality consisted in having discovered them himself (and only when I read the story did I realize all I had come up with). The story concluded with something I'd said about green salsa and the painful chromatics of the Mexican people. For half the price, they could have gotten the same article from me. But we live in a colonial world, and the magazine needed the august signature of Samuel Katzenberg. Plus, I don't write articles.

2. *Burroughs*
The star reporter's return to Mexico tested both my patience and my dignity. How dare he call me?

I told him I had no aspirations to protagonism; I was just sick of Americans taking advantage of us. Instead of translating Monsiváis or Mejía Madrid, they sent a cretin who got the Madonna treatment just because he wrote in English. The planet had turned into a new Babel where nobody could understand anybody else, but the important thing was to not understand anybody else in English.

I thought my speech was patriotic, so I went on and on until I got scared I was sounding anti-Semitic.

"Sorry I didn't mention you," Katzenberg said politely on the other end of the line.

I looked out the window, towards the Parque de la Bola. A little boy had climbed up the enormous cement sphere. He spread his arms, like he was on the top of a mountain. Everyone around him clapped. The Earth had been conquered.

At night, I like to look at the middle of the traffic circle we call the Parque de la Bola, the Ball Park. The ball is a globe made out of concrete. People lean out over their balconies to look at it. The world as seen by its neighbors.

My eyes wandered to the computer, covered with Post-its where I jot down "ideas." At this point, the machine looks like a domesticated Xipe Totec, the Aztec flayed god. Each "idea" is a layer of skin from Our Flayed Father. Instead of writing the script about syncretism I'd already cashed an advance on, I was constructing a monument to the topic.

Katzenberg was trying to win me over.

"The copy editors obliterated crucial adjectives; you know how cutthroat journalism is. Editors over there are not like the ones in Mexico, they're vicious with the red pen, they change everything on you. . . ."

While he was talking, I was thinking about Cristi Suárez. She had left an indelible message on my answering machine. "How's it going with the script? I dreamed about you last night. A nightmare with low-budget slasher effects. You behaved yourself, though: you were the monster, not the one who was chasing me but the one who was saving me. Don't forget we need the first draft by Friday. Thanks for saving me. *Kiss kiss."*

Listening to Cristi is a delectable destruction. I love her proposals on topics I don't like. For her, I've written scripts on genetically modified corn and Brahman cattle ranching. Even though the work is a pretext to get closer to her, I still haven't taken the final step. And it's because up until now, unlikely as it may sound, my best quality has been my scripts. She met me when I was horrendously drunk, but even so, or maybe because of it, she considered me capable of writing a documentary exposing the dangers of transgenic grains. Ever since, she's talked to me as if our previous project had won an Oscar and now we were just gunning for prestige at Cannes. The latest episode of her enthusiasm led me to syncretism. "We Mexicans are pure collage," she said. It's hard to believe, but spoken by her, it sounded sublime.

I'd disconnected my answering machine because I wasn't sure I could handle another message from Cristi and her magnificent nightmares. Sometimes I wonder what I'd have to lose by telling her once and for all that I couldn't care less about syncretism and the only collage I'm interested in is her. But then I remember she likes to take care of people. She thinks of herself as a nurse. Maybe the scripts are the therapy she's assigned to me and all she wants is for me to take my medicine. But the good monster thing sounds racy, almost pornographic. Although it would be more pornographic if she congratulated me on being the bad monster. The soul of a woman is a complicated thing.

Yes, I disconnected the answering machine to erase any record of the voice that obsessed me. When the phone rang twenty times, I couldn't help wondering what kind of psychopath was trying to get hold of me. That's how I ended up talking to Katzenberg again.

He was still on the line. He had run out of polite phrases and was waiting for my response.

I looked in my wallet: two green 200-peso notes, with traces of cocaine (not enough). The sight alone convinced me, but Katzenberg still made an emotional appeal:

"This isn't the first time they've asked me to come back to Mexico. Believe it or not, the Frida story was a hit. I didn't want to come back, and a colleague, an anti-Semitic Irishman who was trying to fuck my girlfriend, spread the rumor that I didn't want to come back because I'd done something dirty. It wouldn't be the first time a gringo reporter got into trouble with the narcotraffickers or the DEA."

"You came back to clear your name?" I asked.

"Yes," he answered, humbly.

I told him I was not "one of the locals." If he wanted to refer to me, he'd have to use my name. It was a question of principles and the proper attribution of sources. Then I asked him for three thousand dollars.

There was a silence on the other end of the line. I thought Katzenberg was doing calculations, but he had already moved on to the subject of his story.

"How violent is Mexico City, really?"

I remembered something Burroughs wrote to Kerouac or Ginsberg or some other big-time addict who wanted to come to Mexico but was scared he'd get jumped.

"Don't worry: Mexicans only kill their friends."

3. *Keiko*

Those days, the only interesting thing in Mexico City was Keiko's farewell. On Sundays, divorced fathers depend heavily on zoos and aquariums. I got in the habit of taking Tania to Adventure Kingdom, the theme park that we thought of as a whale sanctuary.

I decided to spend the morning with Tania, watching the whale swim in powerful circles (my daughter, more accurately, referred to it as an "orca") and in the afternoon I'd look for attractive, violent settings with Katzenberg. That wouldn't be easy. All the spots I've been mugged are too ordinary.

One thing was still unresolved: when would I write that first draft for Cristi?

While I tried to salvage some cocaine dust from a bill with Sor Juana's face on it, I came up with an ontological excuse for my block. What was the point of writing scripts in a country where the Cineteca Theaters exploded while they were showing *The Promised Land?* I remembered the problem we'd had with an extra who got beat up in a scene, and my script had him say *"Aggh!"* The union decided that since the victim had a speaking part, he should be paid as an actor instead of an extra. After that, my victims died in silence.

Anyway, I've never seen the slightest resemblance between what I imagine and the handsome stud or bottle blonde who garbles my words onscreen.

"Why don't you write a novel?" Renata asked me once. We were still married then and she was still willing to change me for my own sake, starting with imagining me as a novelist. "In novels, special effects are free and the characters aren't unionized. All that counts is your inner world."

I'll never forget that phrase. A time actually existed when Renata believed in my inner world. As she spoke those words, she looked at me, with the honey-colored eyes that Tania unfortunately didn't inherit, as if I were a landscape: interesting, but a little out of focus.

None of the accusations she hurled at me later nor any of the fights that led to our divorce hurt me as much as that generous expectation. Her trust was more devastating than the critics. Renata saw in me possibilities I never possessed.

In scripts, "INT" refers to the interior, and mine is decorated with sofas. That's as deep as I go. Anything else is the delusion of a woman who made a mistake searching for depths in me, and who hurt me by believing I was capable of plumbing them myself.

I called Gonzalo Erdiozóbal to ask him to take care of the script. He doesn't write, but his life is like a documentary on syncretism. Before Vienna, he was a veteran of university theater productions (he'd recited Hamlet's monologues waist-deep in a very memorable swamp), he was involved in a freshwater shrimp farming project in Río Pánuco, he left a woman and two children in Saltillo, he financed a video about Monarch butterflies, and he launched a website to give voice to the 62 indigenous communities of Mexico. Plus, Gonzalo is a marvel of practicality. He fixes motors he's never seen before and makes delicious dishes with surprising ingredients he finds in my pantry. His zest for pioneering and love of hobbies are a little annoying, but in times of desperation, there's nothing better. When Renata and I separated, he ignored my pathetic attempts to isolate myself and visited me habitually. He would show up with magazines, videos, and a very hard to find Caribbean rum.

I called Gonzalo and he said he'd never thought about writing a script, which meant yes. I felt so relieved that I got carried away talking. I told him about Katzenberg and his return to Mexico, but he wasn't interested in the journalist's news. He wanted to talk about other things. An old friend from university theater was producing one of Genet's plays in a gymnasium. When Gonzalo describes them, scenes run the risk of lasting as long as they do in real life. I hung up the phone.

I went to pick up Tania. The city was plastered with pictures of the whale. Mexico City is a wonderful place for breeding pandas—the first panda born outside of China was born here—but orcas need more space to start a family. That's why Keiko was leaving. I explained this to my daughter while we waited for one of the goodbye performances to start in Adventure Kingdom's gigantic tank.

Tania had just learned the word "sinister" and she was finding many uses for it. We should have been happy; Keiko would have babies off in the depths. Tania gave me a cross-eyed look. I thought she was going to say it was sinister. I pulled out a picture book she had in her backpack and started to read it to her. It was about carnivorous carrots. She didn't think that was sinister at all.

The whale had been trained to say good-bye to the Mexican people. He waved adiós with his flipper while we sang "The Swallows." A ten-trumpet mariachi band played with enormous sadness, and the singer exclaimed,

"I'm not crying! My eyes are just sweating!"

I confess, I got choked up in spite of myself. I silently cursed Katzenberg, incapable of appreciating the richness of Mexican kitsch. He only paid to see violence.

Keiko leapt from the water one last time. He seemed to smile in a threatening way, with very pointed teeth. On our way out, I bought Tania an inflatable whale.

There were forest fires outside of Ajusco. The ashes brought night on prematurely. From the hill Adventure Kingdom was built on, the city's filthy skin glinted like mica. The perfect backdrop for Cristi's dreams of a good monster.

We got onto the highway without saying a word. I'm sure Tania was thinking about Keiko and the family he would have to travel so far to find.

I dropped Tania off at Renata's house and headed to Los Alcatraces. When I got to the table, it was four in the afternoon. Katzenberg had already eaten.

I'd chosen the restaurant carefully; it was perfect for torturing Katzenberg. I knew he'd thank me for taking him to a genuine locale. They were blasting *ranchera* music, the chairs had that toyshop color-scheme we Mexicans encounter only in "traditional" joints, there were six spicy salsas on the table and the menu offered three kinds of insects. All calamities picturesque enough for my companion to suffer them as "experiences."

Baldness had gained ground on Katzenberg's scalp. He was dressed like a Woolworth's shopper, sporting a shirt with checks in three different colors and a watch with a see-through band. His little eyes, intensely blue, darted around. Eyes faster than flies, on the lookout for an exclusive.

He ordered decaf. They brought him the only coffee they had: *café de olla*, with cinnamon and panela sugar. He barely sipped it. He wanted to be careful about food. He felt a throbbing in his temples, a little sound going *bing-bing.*

"It's the altitude," I assured him. "No one can digest anything at 7500 feet."

He told me about his recent problems. Some colleagues were jealous of him, others hated him for no apparent reason. He had been lucky enough to visit places where conflicts broke out on his arrival and it got him incredible scoops. He was the first one to document the forced relocations in Rwanda, the Kurdish genocide, the toxic gas leak at the Union Carbide factory in India. Everywhere he went, he'd won prizes and made enemies. He felt his adversaries breathing down his neck. We were the same age, 38, but he'd aged in subtle ways, as if he'd crossed all of Africa with no air conditioning. I thought I sensed a bit of pathological lying in the precise enumeration of his grievances. According to him, nobody had forgiven him for being in Berlin the day the wall came down, or for having run into Vargas Llosa in a shirt shop in Paris a week after he'd lost the elections in Peru. I figured he was one of those investigative reporters who brag about the facts they've dug up but lie about their birthdate. Many of the conflicts he'd had with the press must have been sparked by the way he got his stories, taking advantage of people like me.

He eyed the neighboring tables.

"I didn't want to come back to Mexico," he said in a low voice.

Was it possible that someone hardened by coups d'état and radioactive clouds was afraid of the Mexican way of life?

I'd ordered *empipianadas*. Katzenberg looked at my plate as he spoke, as if he were drawing conviction from the thick, green sauce.

"It's an elusive thing. Evil is *transcendent* here. People don't cause harm just because. Evil means something. It was hell, hell that Lawrence Durrell and Malcolm Lowry found in this country. It's a miracle they got out alive. They came into contact with overpowering energies."

Just then, they brought me a clay jug of hibiscus water. The handle had broken off and been taped back on. I gestured at the jug:

"In Mexico, evil is improvised. Don't worry, Samuel."

4. *Oxxo*

Katzenberg's paranoid side was much more likeable. He wasn't the overbearing lion of New Journalism he'd been on his last trip. Whether it was real or imagined, all this intrigue was having a positive effect on him. Now he wanted to write his story and get out fast.

I spoke like only a screenwriter would:

"Is there something I should know?"

He answered like one of my characters:

"What part of what you know don't you understand?"

"You're a nervous wreck. Are you in trouble?

"I already told you about that."

"Are you in trouble you haven't told me about?"

"If I don't tell you something, it's for the good of the mission."

"'The mission.' You sound like a DEA agent."

"Come on," he said, very amused. "I have to protect my source, that's all. I'll tell you what you need to know. You're my Deep Throat. I don't want to lose you."

"Is there something you haven't told me?"

"Yes. Remember the anti-Semitic Irishman?"

"The one who wanted to fuck your girlfriend?"

"That's right. He wanted to fuck my girlfriend because he had already fucked my wife."

"Ah."

"They just named him foreign news editor of *Point Blank.* He knows I haven't been very rigorous with my sources. There's already a price on my head. He's waiting for the tiniest slipup so he can jump on me."

"I thought everyone hated you because you got to Rwanda first."

"There's some of that, too, but with this guy it's all about his uncircumcised dick. Us goddamn gringos have personal problems too. Can you understand that, *güey*?"

"You speak Spanish too well. Everyone here ends up thinking you're CIA."

"I lived here for four years, from 12 to 16, I told you that. I went to school in Mixcoac. Are you going to trust me or not? We need a pact, a marriage of convenience," he smiled.

"They don't teach you to say 'marriage of convenience' at The Mixcoac School."

"There are dictionaries, don't be a jerk. In Mixcoac, I learned what you learn in any high school: to say *güey*, man." He looked at me, his eyes two blue sparks. "Can you understand that I feel like shit, even though I'm paying you three thousand dollars?"

We made peace. I wanted to reward him with some quotidian horror of Mexico in this, the year 2000. I borrowed his phone and dialed up Pancho, a dealer I've considered trustworthy ever since he said to me, "If you want to see the devil smile, give me a call."

Pancho had me meet him two streets away from Los Alcatraces, in the parking lot of an Oxxo minimart. I wanted Katzenberg to see a coke deal, as simple and cheap as ordering Domino's. Routine crime.

Pancho showed up in a grey Camaro, with his little girls in the back. He walked up to my car window, leaned over, dropped a folded-up piece of paper, and pocketed the 200 pesos I palmed him.

"Take care of yourself," he said, an alarming sentiment coming from someone with trembling fingers, a wasted visage, papery skin. Pancho's face was the best antidote against his drugs. The devil wasn't smiling at him. Or maybe that's his secret and bewitching charm, like some poorly-embalmed Phoenician king. Samuel Katzenberg eyed him greedily, extracting adjectives from that ravaged face.

I went into the Oxxo to buy cigarettes. I was at the register when a fast-moving shadow crossed my field of vision. I thought the store was being robbed. But the guy behind the counter looked more curious than horrified. He was watching something going on outside. I turned to look at the parking lot. Katzenberg was being dragged out of my car by a guy in a ski-mask, a Glock held to his head. A second guy in a ski-mask got out of the rear seat of my car, as if he had been searching for something back there. He turned to face all of us watching from inside the store:

"Motherfuckers!"

We didn't need to see him fire. The minute we heard him we dropped to the ground. I went down surrounded by cans, boxes, and a rain of glass. The shot shattered the front window. A second shot shook the building and kept us floored for five minutes.

When I got out of the Oxxo, the doors of my car were still open, infusing it with the helplessness of recently vandalized vehicles. As for Katzenberg, all that remained was a button torn off his jacket in the struggle.

There was a chemical smell, and a cloud of colored smoke drifted towards the sky. The second shot had shattered the two X's of the neon Oxxo sign. Strangely, the other letters were still lit: two glowing circles like drunken eyes.

5. *Buñuel*

Lieutenant Natividad Carmona had very specific ideas:

"If you chew, you think better."

He handed me a pack of blue raspberry gum.

I took one even though I didn't want it.

I sat in the patrol car, an artificial taste in my mouth. From the passenger's seat, Martín Palencia informed his partner:

"El Tamale snuffed it."

Carmona made no comment. I didn't know who El Tamale was, but seeing the news of his death received with such indifference terrified me.

It had taken me a while to react to Katzenberg's kidnapping. That's what happens when you have a slip full of cocaine in your pocket. What do you do when you hear sirens approaching? Pancho sold top-notch product; it would be a crime to dump it.

After searching through my car (in vain, of course), I'd gone back into the Oxxo and headed for the cans of powdered milk. I picked one for infants with acid reflux, the brand that saved Tania when she was a newborn. I pulled off the plastic cap and slipped the paper between the cap and the metal seal. With a little luck, I'd be able to get it back the next day. That milk is a luxury item.

When I got back to the car, there were two cops on the scene. They made a big show of opening the glove compartment and pulling out a baggie of marijuana. While I'd been hiding the coke, they'd been planting this lesser drug in my car. They didn't need it to take me down to the station, but they decided to soften me up just in case. I was about to slip them a bill (with traces of something more incriminating than marijuana on it) when a rat-gray car with lights on its roof screeched to a stop in front of us, its brakes squealing in that magnificent way police cars never seem to pull off in Mexican movies.

That's how I met officers Natividad Carmona and Martín Palencia. They had ferrety hair and manicured fingernails. As I watched them go over the car with deadbeat delight, I noticed a scar on Carmona's forehead and, much more worrying, a Rolex on Palencia's wrist. They treated the uniformed cops with utter disdain. They found my Screenwriters Guild I.D. and the bag of marijuana. I was surprised at how easily they broke it down.

"Look, Daddy-O," Carmona said to one of the cops, "you really think a filmmaker's going to get high on skunk weed like this?" He gestured at me and his voice took on a respectful tone: "The artist is into much finer things." He handed the bag to the cop. "Take that shit away."

The grunt cops took their hopes of extortion elsewhere. I was left in the hands of the Law, trained to sniff out my drug habits from my screenwriter ID.

We were in the parking lot for hours. The officers called Katzenberg's hotel, Interpol, the DEA, and the consular officer at the United States Embassy. Their efficiency turned terrifying when they said,

"Let's go to the holding cells."

I got into the patrol car. It smelled new. The dashboard seemed to have more lights and buttons than were really necessary.

"How close are you and Mr. Katzenberg?" asked Carmona.

I told him what I knew, speaking quickly and stumbling over my words, wanting to fill each sentence with sincerity.

We drove through a neighborhood of low houses. It had rained in this part of the city. Every time we pulled up next to a car, the driver would pretend we weren't there. I've been in that situation hundreds of times: not looking at the Law, trying to pretend it is invisible and will continue along its inscrutable parallel course.

Where could Katzenberg be? Holed up in some shantytown, gagged in some safehouse? I imagined him being dragged by his kidnappers in a series of confusing shots: a back pushing forward into a roiling fog; a body with its hands tied, already lifeless, being dragged through the dirt; a corpse on its way to becoming anonymous, just a faceless victim, the product of a random misunderstanding; an inert mass, licked eagerly by feral dogs.

I imagined an atrocious end for Samuel Katzenberg to avoid thinking about my own. Thirty-eight years in the city is enough to know that a trip to the "holding cells" doesn't always come with a return ticket. *But there are exceptions,* I thought. People who make it through a week eating newspaper in a ditch, people who survive fifteen ice pick wounds, people who are electrocuted in bathtubs full of cold water and live to tell the tale, though nobody believes them. I tried to reassure myself by thinking about hideous possibilities in great detail. I imagined myself deformed but alive, ready to terrify Tania with my embrace. Horrendous, but with the right to a future. Then I wondered if Renata would cry at my funeral. No, she wouldn't even show up at the wake; she wouldn't be able to handle my mother hugging her and saying sad, tender words meant to console her for being guilty for my death.

I wouldn't have sunk into such melodrama if I'd been in clear danger. The patrol car smelled good, I was chewing blue raspberry gum, we were driving along calmly, obeying stoplights. But in some basement somewhere, El Tamale had snuffed it.

"So you're a filmmaker, then?" Martín Palencia asked suddenly.

"I write screenplays."

"Let me ask you this. That Buñuel did every fucking drug, didn't he? I have a ton of movies at home, the pirated stuff we've confiscated from the Tepito black market. All due respect, but I think Buñuel was balls deep. You can tell he was a total druggie, a total visionary. For me, he's the Boss, the Boss of Bosses, like the *Tigres del Norte* say, the kingpin of cinema, the only one who really and truly had square balls." Palencia gestured wildly in support of his theory, and his eyes twinkled, as if he had already spent a lot of time trying to explain this. "Let an old man like that do whatever drugs he wants! I always say, Shakespeare was a fag, what the fuck do I care? Those motherfuckers are creating, creating, creating." He shook his head hard from side to side; the gesture suggested coke or amphetamines. "Do you remember that one that Buñuel did where two chicks are just one chick? They're both hot as hell, but they're different, they don't look a damn thing alike, but an old guy mixes them up, that's how fucked up he is. And neither of them give it up. Those damn girls get hotter and hotter. It's like the old guy was seeing double. It makes you want to be as confused as him. That's surrealism, right? It'd be frickin' cool to live all surrealist!" He paused, and after a deep sigh, asked me, "So what was it, what was Maestro Buñuel into?"

"He liked martinis."

"I told you, partner!" Palencia clapped Carmona on the back.

6. *The Hamster*

After a ride prolonged by a filmic discussion in which Palencia tried to convince Carmona that surrealism was hotter than porn, they left me with an official in the D.A.'s office.

The functionary asked me fifty questions. He asked if I had an alias, and if I had engaged in "sexual commerce" with the kidnapped party.

The tough part of the interrogation wasn't the questions but the way they were repeated, barely modified, to expose any discrepancies. Asked in a different order or in a different tone, the questions suddenly implied something else. They made it seem like I knew about things before they had happened, like I had intuited or even planned them.

I worried about Katzenberg. I had brought him to the Oxxo, so I deserved some of the blame for what had transpired. But something stronger, something distant, dangerous, untraceable, had taken control of him. Would they come after me too? Right now, all I cared about was answering those questions that kept transforming with each repetition. At two in the morning, they let me go.

When I got to my apartment, I collapsed onto the bed, thinking about the cocaine I'd left in the Oxxo. I passed out in my clothes and plunged into a deep sleep, in which I felt the occasional brush of a flipper.

I woke up at eight a.m. and looked out the window at the streets that surround the Parque de la Bola. Then I checked my answering machine. Two messages. Cristi's voice exploded with enthusiasm through the speaker: "The script's a knockout! You're the best. I know compliments are out of style in this post-modern world, don't be offended, but you make me want to be old-fashioned. I'm dying to see you. *Kiss kiss!* Alright, a hundred kisses." Cristi was exultant. I didn't know that Gonzalo

Erdiozábal had sent her the script, nor did I remember giving him Cristi's fax number. Although, honestly, I didn't remember much of anything. The second message said: "Get over here right now. Tania is screaming bloody murder." (My ex-wife always talked to me like our daughter was a burning building and I was 911.)

I had a slice of pound cake and a cigarette for breakfast and left for Renata's place. On the ride over, I thought about Cristi. Her enthusiastic voice, her desire to be old-fashioned. An incredible thing in such a disastrous moment. I wondered if she would ever use that magnificent voice to demand that I come pick up our daughter. Gonzalo had always been a great friend. Now I knew he was also a better screenwriter.

Tania seemed pretty calm when I got there. Renata, on the other hand, glared at me as if she was reading the most abominable crimes all over my face. She shook her hands around like she was trying to swat a cloud of fruit flies. Then she explained the problem: Tania's hamster Lobito had gotten lost in the Chevrolet, the run-down piece of crap that's caused us so many problems and is rolling proof that the alimony I send her is bare-bones. She pointed at the car: a chance for me to do my part, problems men should fix.

I searched the car for the hamster, imitating some of the expert moves I'd seen the detectives use. The only thing I found was a tortoiseshell brooch shaped like an infinity symbol. Renata had been wearing it when I met her. It was just as hard for me to believe such thin, translucent material could come from a turtle as it was to believe my fingers had once unpinned it from her. Now the clasp was stuck—or my fingers had lost the touch.

I decided to bring some specialists in on the search for Lobito. Tania went with me to the Chevrolet dealership. A mechanic in a white lab coat listened blankly to my request, as if customers came by every day with rodents lost in the chassis of their cars.

"Wait in Customer Service." He pointed to a glass-walled rectangle.

There we went. The nation's waiting rooms have filled up with televisions; we sat and watched a commercial for the government that I found especially repugnant because I was the one who'd written it. For a full minute, it shows an imaginary country where four cinderblock walls count for a classroom and the president smiles, satisfied with his achievements. The message couldn't be any more contradictory: poverty seems to be simultaneously resolved and undefeatable. The shot pulls out to show a barren landscape. It's as if the government were saying, "We've done what little we could." The last image is a miserable little boy with his mouth open under an eyedropper. Executive authority lets a single, provident drop fall in.

I kept my eyes closed until Tania tugged on my pants.

The man in the white coat had Lobito in his hands:

"We had to take apart the back seat." He handed Tania her pet. "We found this, too." He passed me a tennis ball that had lost its bright lime color in the dark recesses of the car.

I took it with trembling hands. Its fuzzy texture triggered unsettling memories: Gonzalo Erdiozábal, unrepentant faker, had betrayed me.

7. *The Blesséd Baby Mechanic*

In the Eighties, Renata had wanted to live unhindered, but she also needed a car. Though she hated the idea of a man protecting her, she let her father buy her a Chevrolet. For a few weeks, she felt like a traitor and a dependent. She kept throwing her three little I Ching coins into the air but she couldn't find any metaphors to reassure her.

Always happy to help a friend, and to have an excuse to make his generosity a performance, Gonzalo Erdiozábal convinced her to get the car blessed in a traditional rite: "Daddy's present" could be transformed into a "sacramental ride."

Gonzalo had such an intense way of being incoherent that we accepted his plan. We would go see a priest known for blessing taxis on the day of St. Christopher, patron saint of travelers. The church was very far away, but it would be worth it to take a little trip, try something different for a change.

Renata never wanted to baptize Tania. But pulling up to the Anthropology Department in a brand new car made her feel guilty; an automotive baptism seemed like her chance to mix a bourgeois gift with a socially commended act.

Gonzalo appointed himself godfather. He showed up at our house with a cooler full of beer and snacks from the Tlalpan market.

We went to the outer limits of the city, and even that far out, amazingly, the city kept going. We got lost more than once along the way. Nobody seemed to have heard of the parish, and we kept getting contradictory directions until finally we saw a taxi decked out for a party, covered with crepe-paper flowers, and decided to follow it.

When we got there, dozens of taxis were waiting to be baptized. In the back was the chapel with its little marshmallow-blue towers, like a kindergarten converted into a church.

"Do you think they'll baptize a car if it's not a taxi?" Renata asked.

"That's the important thing: not being a taxi, and being here," Gonzalo spoke like a guru of the hybrid world.

He hired a trio of mariachis to play for us while we waited. We sat listening to *boleros*, and after my fourth beer, I started to feel bad for my friend. I've left out a crucial detail: Gonzalo was desperately, shamelessly in love with Renata. His flirting was so obvious that it didn't even bother me. While we listened to a *bolero* proposing a million ways to suffer from love, I thought about the emptiness that defined Gonzalo's life and determined his ever-shifting hobbies, how every year for him was constant forward-motion, constant flight.

There was the occasional woman. None lasted long enough to knit him a vest in psychedelic colors or for him to master a new yoga pose. Renata had been a perpetually-postponed horizon, a way to justify his empty flings.

Waiting in line, I felt intensely sorry for Gonzalo and told him the sorts of things that you say in between romantic songs, until the chords come back in to collect their due.

The trio ran out of songs before we reached the chapel. When we were finally just three taxis away, they told us that the water had run out, too, not only in the church but in the whole neighborhood.

We looked at the priest's dry holy water sprinkler. The wind sent newspapers and plastic bags into the sky.

Renata resigned herself to the idea of driving a car in limbo and parking in the Anthropology Department without having gone through a vernacular rite.

Gonzalo was drunk by then and entirely committed to being our automotive godfather. He told us to wait for him, and disappeared down a dirt road.

We went into the church. On a side altar, we saw the Blesséd Baby Mechanic. His cross was a lug wrench; he was swaddled in a denim jumpsuit. The little pink face, with its fuchsia cheeks, was sloppily painted.

The altar was surrounded by painted tin votive offerings giving thanks for highway miracles and tiny cars the taxi drivers left as offerings.

We went out into the atrium and stood under the last rays of afternoon sun.

Gonzalo had set off with the look of one possessed. I pitied his solitude, his vicarious passion for Renata, his useless costume changes.

A loud bang and a cloud of dust announced his return. He pulled up, hanging out the cab of an Electropura Purified Water delivery truck. The glass bottles sparkled blue in the setting sun.

Up to that point the image was epic, or at least bizarre. When we got closer, it became criminal: Gonzalo was threatening the driver with the metal pin-punch he used to carve *Peace & Love* signs into balsa wood. When he got out of the truck, his face had the deformed look of the demented.

The priest refused to perform the sacrament with stolen water.

Gonzalo showed him a fistful of bills:

"He refused to sell me a bottle."

"I'm not authorized to go off my route," said the truck driver, in a slavish tone closed to all suggestions.

"This water has already been suffused with sin," declared the priest.

In the dusty air, the bottles shone like treasure.

"Please!" Gonzalo got down on his knees with a grand pathos directed as much at the truck driver as the priest.

Two taxi drivers helped us get him into the car. He didn't speak the whole ride back. Our outlandish Saturday fun had turned into something shameful. More than anything, it was awful to be unable to console our friend. After my most embarrassing coke-fueled episodes, he'd told me, "Don't worry, it happens to everyone." Effectively, anyone could become a lamentable addict. I couldn't say the same thing to him. His loss of control was unique.

I walked him to the door of his building. He hugged me tightly. I could smell his sour sweat.

"I'm sorry, I'm a terrible friend," he mumbled.

Obviously, I thought he was referring to our absurd expedition to the St. Christopher church. Years later, the tennis ball found under the back seat would tie things together differently.

8. *The Motto*

A few weeks before the failed baptism, we spent a weekend with several other couples at the hacienda of Giménez

Luque, a millionaire friend of ours. Even though our host was the only one who really knew how to swing a racquet, the tennis court drew us in like an attainable oasis. More than a few balls went sailing over the metal grille that enclosed the court. But only one of them matters: the one Renata and Gonzalo went after. They came back more than an hour later, empty-handed. They'd looked everywhere for it, but couldn't figure out where it had gone. Renata was flushed. She chewed obsessively at a hang-nail on her index finger.

Now I knew the truth: they hadn't lost the ball in the field outside the court, they'd lost it in the back seat of the Chevrolet, from where they'd just emerged. The same spot my comb had fallen into when Renata and I had made love in the Leones Desert! Lobito had ended up in the very same place.

Could it be some other ball? Absolutely not. The number of lost tennis balls in the world is impossible to imagine. But the feeling I had when I touched the fuzz of that ball, so recently exposed, was irrefutable.

Plus, there were other clues. My relationship with Renata had begun to cool around the same time. She didn't want to make love to me at the hacienda. Her hands avoided mine.

Renata was never interested in tennis again, after that. It's possible that she was no longer interested in Gonzalo, either. I can't find any later connections between them. In a way, she divorced both of us. She couldn't imagine one friend without the other. Gonzalo was, for her, what he had been so many times for others, and for himself: a fit of passion, essential and brief.

Either way, Gonzalo had crossed the line into being a complete son of a bitch. When he apologized to me outside his house, he wasn't referring to the ridiculousness of that Saturday, but to a betrayal he couldn't speak.

The tennis ball burned in my hand. I was so enraged I couldn't think about anything else for the rest of the day. I forgot the cocaine I had left in the Oxxo. I forgot Katzenberg had disappeared. I forgot that Tania's inflatable whale needed a tank.

I tried in vain to find Erdiozábal. I set the Post-its covering my computer on fire, one by one, just to do something. They burned like sacrificial skins, but I didn't feel any better.

I flipped through magazines. In a *Rolling Stone* from two years ago, I found an interview with Katzenberg I hadn't seen before. The reporter asked him, "What's your motto?" Curiously, he had one: "Float in the depths." Maybe that's what being successful means, having a motto. I burned the last yellow Post-it and went out into the street.

The Parque de la Bola wasn't the best place to clear my mind. Martín Palencia, the surreal-cinefile detective, was there. He was holding the sports section and a cappuccino in a Styrofoam cup. He'd been just about to take a little break before knocking on my door. My arrival ruined it for him.

He talked reluctantly about the things they'd found in Katzenberg's hotel room: notes on violence, "express kidnapping", ATM "milking," people who'd been "trunked" in cars. What did I know about it? I told him Katzenberg had wanted to write about sinister things but hadn't yet run into any; his editors in New York were demanding he find something horrifying in Mexico, an atrocity theme-park.

Palencia sipped his cappuccino, absorbed in his own thoughts.

I remembered Katzenberg's pretentious motto. Now he'd need it for real. Would he be able to float in the depths he'd fallen into? I repeated what I knew, which was almost nothing.

Palencia mentioned with pointed interest that the word "Buñuel-esque" appeared in Katzenberg's notes. Was it a clue, or what?

"When a gringo journalist finds something 'Buñuel-esque' in Mexico, it means that he saw something horrible he thought was magical."

"Doesn't it occur to you that this could be a conspiracy?" He suddenly switched to the informal, threateningly: "The gringo was here to see you, don't forget. If you get cute, you're gonna get fucked. Do you remember the Buñuel film, *The Criminal Life of Archibaldo de la Cruz?*"

"Yes," I answered, to hurry along the dialogue.

"Remember what happens to the blonde's mannequin: it gets burned to a crisp. Then the leading lady gets burned to a crisp. Blondes who don't talk end up in flames, sweetheart."

I wanted to make my exit, but Palencia stopped me:

"Don't get lost, now." He touched my cheek with homicidal affection.

I went back to my building. Cristi was standing at the door.

"Sorry for dropping by unannounced. I was dying to see you." Her eyes sparkled more than usual; she ran her hand through her hair nervously. "I'm not always like this, really."

We went up to my apartment. The first thing she did was look at my computer, recently cleared of its Post-it leaf litter.

"I love the idea you start the script with: the computer covered in Post-its, like a modern-day Xipe Totec. You can feel the desperation of the screenwriter and the contemporary manifestation of syncretism. But I'm not here to get pedantic." She took my hand.

Gonzalo Erdiozábal had made me the protagonist of his script. His abusive imagination never ceased to amaze me, but I couldn't go on thinking. Cristi's lips were grazing mine.

9. *Barbie*

The classy thing would have been to forget my 200 pesos' worth of cocaine, but I went back to the Oxxo prepared to go through every single can of acid-reflux formula. Not a single one was left.

"The pollution gives babies reflux," the cashier told me. "We never have enough cans."

Gonzalo was just as impossible to find as my cocaine. I left him multiple messages. In return, he recorded a terse message on my answering machine: "I've been running around like crazy. I'm going to Chiapas with some Swedish Human Rights guys. Good luck with the script."

At that point, we hadn't heard anything about Keiko, either. Had he reached the open sea yet? I made the

mistake of going back to Adventure Kingdom with
Tania. A listless dolphin was swimming circles in
the tank.

Now I was worried about Katzenberg and afraid that
Palencia would return to make me the fall guy for a crime I
knew nothing about. But what I was most distressed about,
I admit, was not knowing what "I" had written. Cristi loved
the personality Gonzalo had captured in the script.

I knew she had an exquisite mole halfway down her
ribs, and a unique way of flicking her tongue in my ear,
but I didn't know how I had wooed her. Even though
she insisted she'd been into me from the beginning,
it was the script that really did it. Plus, the script let
her feel like she'd had a hand in the way I'd opened
up: she had suggested the topic. Her pride seemed
well-deserved to me. I just needed to find out what her
admiration was based on. She quoted phrases from the
script with such frequency that when she said "God is
a concept by which we measure our pain," I thought it
was something that "I" had written. She had to explain,
with humiliating pedantry, that she was quoting John
Lennon.

Either Gonzalo's text was very long, or my interior
was very sparse. According to Cristi, it showed me in
my entirety. She was especially amazed by my bravery
in confessing my flaws and my emotional shortcomings.
It was admirable that I'd been able to overcome them
through Mexican syncretism: "I" represented the country
with astonishing sincerity.

Cristi was in love with the suffering, convincing character created by Gonzalo, the shadow of which I tried to

imitate without a script to follow. Would it be going too far to ask Cristi for a copy?

I began a vague program of personal reform. Spurred by the mysterious virtues Cristi attributed to me, I cut back on sordid mornings with bills up my nose. Life without coke isn't easy, but little by little I was convincing myself to be a different man, complete with sudden tics and old-fashioned courtesy, to distinguish me from the absurd person I had been so far.

The Katzenberg case was still open, and I had to go back to the Police Headquarters. My statements were counter-checked against the ones given by the other witnesses and the Oxxo cashier. A one-eyed agent took down everything we said. He wrote incredibly quickly, as if he had access to abilities beyond the grasp of people with two eyes.

When compared, our statements—mangled, dubious, reticent—gave a violent sense of unreality, of almost purposeful contradictions. There were discrepancies in time and points of view. It didn't do any good for me to say, "In this country, nobody knows anything."

They detained me longer than the others. After seven hours, one fact became clearer and clearer in my mind until it fit within the judicial range of "evidence:" when we left Los Alcatraces, I had used Katzenberg's phone to tell Pancho we were on our way. Then I'd left it in the back seat of the car. I hadn't given it back to him. That's what the second kidnapper was looking for. They wanted Katzenberg with his phone.

I was excited to find a missing piece amidst the chaos, but I didn't tell the one-eyed agent. The phone was proof of my ties to cocaine trafficking.

I was exhausted, but Officer Martín Palencia still wanted to talk to me. Natividad Carmona stood a few feet away, watching and eating a green Jell-O.

"Take a look." He showed me a Barbie doll. "This is one of the ones assembled in Tuxtepec, but they put *Made in China* on them. It was in Mr. Katzenberg's room. Do you know why?"

"A gift for his daughter, I guess."

"Would you buy a Barbie in Mexico if you were a gringo? This is really getting to be like *The Criminal Life of Archibaldo de la Cruz*, oh, yes, it is."

Palencia came over to me:

"Look, sweet thing. You can be a filmmaker without being a whore. I'm not at the point where I want you to suck my cock, but if you gave weird information to your gringo daddy, you're gonna regret it. Bad girls get real fucked." He opened the Barbie's legs; his index finger looked like an enormous penis. "I don't want to have to tear you in half, dolly girl." It was clear he wasn't talking to the Barbie.

When they finally let me go, Carmona was chewing on an orange peel.

10. *Sharon*

Two days later a blonde entered the scene, though not the kind that Palencia was expecting. Sharon came to Mexico to look for her husband. She came in shorts, like she was visiting the palm-tree tropics. That outfit, and every other outfit of hers I saw, was quite unflattering on someone that overweight. On her feet, the reluctant Nikes didn't seem sporty so much as orthopedic.

I had a late breakfast with Sharon and left with a head-
ache. She was annoyed that there were so many smoking
tables, that the music was so loud, that televisions were
omnipresent decorations. All of that annoys me too, but
I don't get hysterical about it. She was surprised that
we Mexicans only know about yellow American cheese
(apparently there's also a white one, much healthier)
and that I couldn't tell her which of the three rolls they
offered us had the most fiber. Her nutritional obsessions
were pathological (considering how fat she was) and her
cultural habits were put on no less severe a diet. To make
conversation, I asked if her husband's kidnapping was
being reported on CNN.

"Television is the same as a frontal lobotomy. I never
watch it," she responded.

From the little she had seen of Mexico City, she was
convinced we don't respect the blind. I told her the best
way to tolerate this city is to be blind, but she didn't
appreciate the joke.

"I'm talking about the handicapped," she said solemnly.
"There are no ramps. Crossing a street is a savage act."

Even though she was right, it annoyed me that she'd
make generalizations like that, having seen so few streets.
I fell into a stony silence. She showed me the latest issue
of *Point Blank*, with an article on Katzenberg: "Missing:
Desaparecido."

I already disliked Sharon so much that I had no problem reading right in front of her. Between childhood
photos and the testimonies of his friends, the journalist
was evoked as a martyr to freedom of expression, meeting his end in a lawless wilderness. Mexico City provided

a harrowing background for the article, a labyrinth ruled
by petty tyrants and gods that should have never crawled
out of the earth.

I was annoyed by the doctored beatification of the
journalist, but I took his side when Sharon said,

"Sammy's no action hero. Do you know how many
laxatives he takes a day?" She paused, and I was unsur-
prised when she added, "We were about to separate. I see
a weird angle in all of this. Maybe he ran off with someone else, maybe he's afraid to face my lawyers."

I didn't have a very high opinion of Katzenberg, but
his wife was arguing that he had kidnapped himself.

Sharon looked over at the table next to us. Within
minutes, she found ten things wrong with the way in
which those parents were raising their child.

I don't know if Sharon was fortified by America's
Puritan traditions—pioneers who had defeated the fierce
elements, undecorated churches where they sang hymns
in pious simplicity, daily lives full of prayer. What I do
know is she was convinced that horrible truth is more
conclusive. She acted on the outskirts of emotional con-
siderations, as if by separating feelings from acts, she
was fulfilling an ethical end.

Over dessert, which unfortunately did not include
low-calorie cookies, she extrapolated her ethics. If she
gave in to feeling, everything would be lost. She could
only be guided by principles.

She had sued *Point Blank* for publishing photos from the
family album without permission. The photos had hurt her
interests: once they got out, it would be more difficult to sell
an exclusive for a miniseries about her husband's tragedy.

She had come from Los Angeles, where she had been talking with producers. I could be helpful. Obviously, nobody would accept a Mexican screenwriter. Would I be interested in a consulting position? Saying no had never been so sweet.

"I'm Samuel's friend," I lied.

11. *La Bola is the World*

The nightmare of having to see Sharon was offset by Cristi's unprecedented acts of love. She took Sharon to the Saturday Bazaar to buy traditional crafts, got her some drops that instantaneously disinfected salads, and gave her a list of 24-hour pharmacies.

Plus, she was getting on great with Tania. She memorized the story about the carnivorous carrots so she could recite it for her during traffic jams.

The most surprising thing was that Cristi's abundant good vibes even made their way to Renata. They ran into each other one afternoon outside my apartment.

"Your girlfriend's so cute," said my ex.

For a moment, I thought that I too might be capable of "floating in the depths."

But one night, while I was drifting off watching the news, the phone rang.

"I'm here." Hearing that voice, trembling, subdued, barely audible, meant understanding, with hair-raising clarity, "I'm alive."

"Where is 'here'?" I asked him.

"In the Parque de la Bola."

I put on my shoes and crossed the street. Samuel Katzenberg stood next to the cement sphere. He looked thinner. Even in the darkness, his eyes reflected anguish. I hugged his checkered shirt. He wasn't expecting that; he seemed startled. Then, as if he were only now learning how to do it, he put his arms around me. He wept, with a hollow moan. A man walking an Afghan crossed the street when he noticed us.

Katzenberg smelled like rancid flesh. Between sobs, he told me they had let him go on the outskirts of town, near a cement factory. He'd flagged down a cab. He didn't remember my address, but he did remember the absurd name of the traffic circle across the street.

"Parque de la Bola," he recited.

He fell silent. Then he looked at the cement sphere, walked up to it, laid his stiffened hands on its surface, recognizing the weak contours of the continents.

"*La bola* is the world," he said intensely.

We went up to my apartment. After he had showered, he told me that he'd been hooded and kept in a tiny closet. The only food they gave him was cereal. One time, they put hallucinogenic mushrooms in it. They took off his hood once a day so he could contemplate an altar covered in a strange combination of images: Catholic, pre-Hispanic, postmodern. A Virgin of Guadalupe, an obsidian knife, dark sunglasses. In the afternoons, they played "The End" by the Doors, for hours and hours. Behind him, someone imitated the anguished, drugged-out voice of Jim Morrison. The torture had been terrible, but it had helped him understand the Mexican apocalypse.

Katzenberg's eyes darted from side to side, like he was looking for someone else in the room. I didn't have to look. It was obvious who had kidnapped him.

12. *Friendly Fire*

"Miracle of miracles!" Gonzalo Erdiozábal answered the door in his slippers.

I walked into his apartment without saying a word. It took some time before I could speak. Too many things were swirling around in my interior, that place I take such care to avoid when I write screenplays. When I finally started talking, I couldn't convey the complexity of my emotions.

Gonzalo sat on a sofa upholstered with mini carpets. The decor made manifest its owner's textile hysteria. There were Huichol weavings in colors evoking the mental electricity of peyote, and Afghan rugs, and paintings by an ex-girlfriend who got her fifteen minutes of fame by threading horse hairs through amate paper.

"Care for some tea?" offered Gonzalo.

I didn't give him the chance to play herbalist. I glanced at the poster of Morrison on the wall. The kidnapping had his patented design. How could he be so callous? He had made his victim kneel in front of a syncretic altar that might—and the idea terrified me—have appeared in "my" screenplay.

With sincere and clumsy words, I talked about his taste for manipulation. We weren't his friends. We were his pawns. We could go to jail because of him! The detectives had me under surveillance! If he didn't give a damn about me, he could at least have thought of Tania. A bitter taste filled my mouth. I didn't want to look at Gonzalo. I concentrated on the arabesques in the main rug.

"I'm sorry," he said, repeating the phrase that had, once again, proven him guilty. "I'm not asking you to understand. But every story has two sides. Let me tell mine."

I let him tell it, not because I wanted to but because my lips were trembling too much for me to refuse.

He reminded me that on Samuel Katzenberg's last visit, he had invented Mexican rituals at my behest. It was me who'd got him involved with the journalist. Martín Palencia had been right when he'd caressed the doll's blonde hair: I had connected Katzenberg with his kidnapper, though I didn't know it at the time. Why hadn't I figured it out sooner? What kind of moron was I, next to Gonzalo?

"I'm an actor," he said in a calm voice. "I always have been, you know that. The thing is, theater got too small for me, so I started to look for other forums. You didn't introduce me to Samuel so I'd tell him the truth, you introduced me so that I would simulate it."

Katzenberg had grown fond of Gonzalo, and told him when he was coming back to Mexico. He told Gonzalo before he told me. That's why Gonzalo wasn't surprised when I mentioned that the journalist was returning to the city. Was it wrong for Gonzalo to get back in touch with Katzenberg on his own? No, of course not. Samuel had been frank with him: his marriage was falling apart, and the pre-nup had a clause that freed him of all responsibility if he suffered a severe nervous breakdown. Plus, he needed to write a good story.

"There was no anti-Semitic Irishman fucking his girlfriend and his wife. Samuel doesn't have a girlfriend. Have you met Sharon? That proves the Irishman doesn't exist. Sammy likes set-ups, too. He wanted to have you on his side. He thinks you're sentimental. Do you know why he needed to write a good story? Because the fact checker screwed him over when he published the article on Frida Kahlo and the volcano. The fact checker found all kinds of exaggerations and lies, but he didn't correct any of it. Two years later, there was a 'fact audit.' That sort of thing happens in the United States. They're freaking truth-Puritans. A battalion of fact checkers went over the stories and Sammy got caught with his pants down. The principle source of his garbage was you. You told him all kinds of bullshit to placate his need for exoticism. Samuel was wrong: his Deep Throat was delirious. Do you know why he went looking for you on his second visit? So he would know what *not* to write about. You're the original faker. Accept it, jackass."

That's what Katzenberg thought of me: my words represented the outer limits of credibility. That's why he seemed so elusive and unsure at Los Alcatraces. He wasn't distrusting the other tables, he was distrusting what was right in front of him.

The kidnapping orchestrated by Gonzalo immersed Katzenberg in the reality he so yearned for. Katzenberg had lived it as something indisputably true: his days in captivity were devastatingly authentic.

"In war, sometimes a commando will hit his own troops. They call it friendly fire, *amigo*. I don't think Samuel suffered any more than he wanted to suffer. The divorce and the story were handed to him on a platter. Do you know who paid his ransom?" He took a theatrical pause. "His magazine."

"How much did they give you, you son of a bitch?"

"Let me finish: do you know what Samuel uncovered?"

I didn't answer. My mouth was full of bitter spit.

"Do you know about the Tuxtepec Barbies?" he asked me.

I thought about the doll the detective had shown me, but I didn't say anything. Gonzalo needed no response from me to keep talking:

"Before he spoke to you, Samuel went to Tuxtepec. He discovered a factory full of Chinese workers. A Shanghai mafia was falsifying Mexican toys that were purportedly coming from Peking. We live in a world of ghosts: copies of copies, everything is pirated. Samuel's next story is going to be called 'Chinese Shadows.'"

Gonzalo Erdiozábal poured himself a cup of tea.

"You sure you don't want any?"

"Is it pirated tea?" I asked. "How much did you get out of them?"

"What kind of insect do you think I am? I didn't get anything. Those 75,000 dollars are for the poor children of Chiapas."

He showed me a receipt printed in a language I couldn't read. Then he added,

"The Swedish government is going to supervise the deposits. We're giving violence a run for its money, for a good cause." He sipped his tea slowly, opening a parenthesis to add, "You confused poor Samuel with all that bullshit you told him last time. He almost lost his job. He didn't know who to trust. If I hadn't kidnapped him, the Chinese Mafia would have done him in."

"You kidnapped him philanthropically?"

"Don't oversimplify. In the end it was all for a good cause."

I couldn't take it any more:

"Do you think fucking Renata was a good cause?"

"What are you talking about?"

"About the hacienda, asshole. About the tennis court. About when you went with Renata to look for a ball and took forever to come back. I'm talking about the ball that I just found in the back seat of a Chevrolet, the Chevrolet where you fucked Renata. You're an animal."

Gonzalo was about to answer when his phone started ringing. The ring tone was Jimi Hendrix's cover of the U.S. national anthem.

Bizarrely, Gonzalo said,

"It's for you." He handed me the phone.

It was Cristi. She had searched heaven, earth, and sea for me. She missed me unbearably. She missed the wrinkles around my eyes. Gunslinger wrinkles. That's what she said. A gunslinger who kills everybody but is still the good guy of the movie.

Gonzalo Erdiozábal watched me from behind the cloud of steam that was rising from his tea.

When I hung up, he spoke in a weak voice.

"I made a mistake with Renata. It didn't help anybody: not you, not her, not me. You two were falling apart. Admit it. I was the exit sign, nothing more. I apologized. Years ago. Do you want me to get down on my knees? I don't mind. I'm sorry, *güey*. I fucked up with Renata, but not with Cristi."

"What are you trying to say?"

"She adores you. I knew it from the day we ran into her

on our way out of that awful play, *The Lizards' Corner.* All she needed was a push. She had her doubts about you. Well, we all have our doubts about you, but at least that's something, most people I have no doubt about. Most people are awful and that's it."

"Did you take her out to play tennis, too?"

"Don't be banal. I wrote what I think of you, which apparently is marvelous. No? I did it in first person, as if it were you talking. I'm an actor; first person sounds very sincere in the voice of actors."

I didn't respond to that. It cost me a lot to say the words, but I couldn't leave without asking:

"Do you have a copy of the script?"

"Of course, Maestro."

Gonzalo seemed to have been waiting for me to ask. He handed me a spiral-bound folder.

"Do you like the cover? The texture is called 'smoke.' It's black but you can see through it—like your mind. Read it so you can see how much I love you."

Some remnant of dignity kept me from responding.

I left without the melodrama of slamming the door, but couldn't resist the minor offense of leaving it open.

13. *Dollars*

Katzenberg went back to New York with his wife, but he got divorced a few weeks later, without any legal hiccups. Anyone who gets kidnapped in Mexico and is declared by the president to be "an American hero" is entitled to his pre-nup exception clause.

He called me from his new apartment, very grateful for what I had done for him.

"I misjudged you after my first trip. Gonzalo insisted that I contact you again. It really was worth it."

His story about Chinese pirated goods was a success, soon surpassed by the chronicle of his kidnapping, which won the Meredith Non-Fiction Award.

With the same breathlessness as Katzenberg's American readers, I read the script Gonzalo had forged for me with defiant precision. He had drawn a perfect pantomime of my manias, but he managed to make my limitations seem brilliant and interesting. His autobiography of me was a display of his actor's skill at forgery, but also of the tolerance with which he had borne my flaws. He had a strange way of being a great friend, but he really was.

On account of my pride, it took me two months to tell him so.

I never said anything to Renata about her affair with Gonzalo. My only act of vengeance was to give her the tennis ball I found in the Chevrolet, though memory is a capricious universe. Indifferently, she took it and put it in a fruit basket, like just one more apple.

Cristi was getting along better and better with Tania, although she didn't share our interest in Keiko, maybe because that had started before she came into our lives.

Only the news about the whale was sad: he didn't know how to hunt, he hadn't found a mate in the icy seas. He seemed to miss his aquarium in Mexico City. The only good thing—at least for us—was that he was going to star in the movie *Free Willy*.

"Why don't you write the script?" Tania asked me, with that heartrending belief in me her mother had felt, years before.

Cristi was right, the time had come to forget the orca.

The final episode related to Samuel Katzenberg occurred one afternoon while I was contemplating the Parque de la Bola and the children skateboarding around the miniature world. The sky shone clean. Finally, the forest fires were over. A whisper sent me over to the door. Somebody had slipped an envelope underneath it.

I guessed what it was from its weight: not a letter, not a book. I opened the envelope carefully. Along with the dollars, there was a message from Samuel Katzenberg. "I'll be coming to Mexico in the next few days, for another story. Is this good for an advance?"

Half an hour later, the phone rang. Katzenberg, for sure. The air filled with the tension of unanswered phone calls. But I didn't pick up.